Praise for

The Prodigal Father

I am very impressed with *The Prodigal Father*. I loved the character development. I feel like I know these people. I was caught up in the story from the very first chapter and wanted to read more.

—Sherie Murphy

Richard Siddoway is a master storyteller. *The Prodigal Father* is a powerful tale of the importance of honesty, the possibility of change, and the hope of reconciliation. It is a positive and helpful read. I recommend it!

—Don H. Staheli, author of the children's best-seller, *The Story of the Walnut Tree*

It was almost shocking how quickly I became emotionally invested in this story. Expertly written and full of achingly real characters, *The Prodigal Father* is a truly heartwarming tale of sorrow, forgiveness, and redemption that stayed with me long after I finished it. Simply a joy to read.

—Lauren Winder Farnsworth, CPA, author of *Chasing Red*, *Catching Lucas Riley*, and *Keeping Kate*

The Prodigal Father is more than just a fable; it's an intricately woven story whose richly developed characters learn through their mistakes and trials that through the Savior's love, all is not lost. They—and we—can ultimately become the people we are meant to be.

—Laura L. Walker, author of *The Matchup*

THE PRODIGAL FATHER

A NOVEL

RICHARD M. SIDDOWAY

New York Times Bestselling Author

THE PRODIGAL FATHER

A NOVEL

Does it take a funeral to learn how to forgive?

BONNEVILLE BOOKS
An Imprint of Cedar Fort, Inc.
Springville, Utah

ISBN 13: 978-1-4621-1963-9

Published by Bonneville Books, an imprint of Cedar Fort, Inc., 2373 W. 700 S., Springville, UT 84663
Distributed by Cedar Fort, Inc. www.cedarfort.com

LIBRARY OF CONGRESS CATALOGING-IN-PUBLICATION DATA

Names: Siddoway, Richard M., author.
Title: The prodigal father / Richard M. Siddoway.
Description: Springville, Utah : Bonneville Books, an imprint of CFI, Inc.,
  [2017]
Identifiers: LCCN 2016058810 | ISBN 9781462119639 (perfect bound)
Subjects: LCSH: Domestic fiction. | GSAFD: Christian fiction.
Classification: LCC PS3569.I29 P76 2017 | DDC 813/.54--dc23
LC record available at https://lccn.loc.gov/2016058810

Cover design by Shawnda T. Craig
Cover design © 2017 by Cedar Fort, Inc.
Edited and typeset by Erica Myers

Printed in the United States of America

10 9 8 7 6 5 4 3 2 1

Printed on acid-free paper

ALSO BY RICHARD M. SIDDOWAY

Christmas of the Cherry Snow

An Honest Heart

Degrees of Glory

The Christmas Quest

The Hut in the Tree in the Woods

The Christmas Wish

Habits of the Heart

Mom and Other Great Women I've Known

Twelve Tales of Christmas

The Cottage Park Puzzle

To Sharlene, Becca, Sherri, Kati, Stan,
Derick, Brett, and David

PART ONE

Homecoming

CHAPTER 1

Friday, December 18, 2015

Scott sat in his truck and watched the quarter-sized snowflakes falling softly. A couple of inches had gathered on the lawn—a white contrast to the tan tufts of December grass that poked through here and there. He'd been there nearly half an hour watching the people enter and exit the church while trying to sum up the courage to go inside. Despite the refrigerator coldness of his ten-year-old Ford pickup, his forehead was beaded with sweat. The windshield kept fogging, and he'd cleared it a half dozen times with a swipe of the back of his hand.

Thirty-two years, he thought. *Thirty-two years since I last walked into that chapel.* He glanced at his watch—7:55—the viewing was supposed to end in five minutes. He took a deep breath, undid his seat belt, and pushed the door open. He slid out from under the steering wheel, smoothed down the front of his pants with his sweat-slicked palms, and walked through the swirling flakes toward the church. It was the first time he'd worn a suit since . . . well, that was another part of his life. He was surprised it still fit him, although it was a little tighter than he remembered. Snowflakes gathered on his shoulders and he brushed them off. Someone had spread ice melt on the sidewalk, and his shoes crunched through the blue and white crystals.

An older couple approached the door just in front of him; the man held the door for his wife and continued to hold it for Scott.

"Thank you." A puffy cloud surrounded the words before he entered the warmth of the building.

"My pleasure," the white-haired gentleman answered. He leaned forward and looked at Scott's face through his glasses. "Scotty Simms. Is that you?"

Scott inhaled as his gaze dropped to the floor. It had been ages since anyone had called him Scotty. "I'm afraid so."

"It has been such a long time. You probably don't remember me. I'm Brother Myers. I used to be your scoutmaster." He extended his hand and took Scott's. The handclasp was firm and friendly. "I'm so sorry about your father. He was such a good man."

Bile rose in Scott's throat and he was unsure what to say. At last he blurted out, "Thank you."

Brother and Sister Myers moved down the hallway toward the Relief Society room. *The carpet used to be orange,* Scott thought, *now it's blue—times change.* His resolve to be here dissolved like the snow-flakes that clung to his shoulders. He hung back next to the exit door. The Myerses paused at a small table holding a book for visitors to sign. Next to it was a longer table covered with a white cloth. Mementos from his father's life were carefully arranged on its surface. Scott stood motionless, examining it from a distance. He exhaled sharply and with a shake of his head, turned to leave.

At that moment, the outside door opened again, letting in a blast of cold air and a swirl of snowflakes. Scott stepped out of the way as another couple entered the church. In their late forties, they exuded the aroma of wealth. The woman turned and looked at Scott, nodded her head gently, and followed her husband down the hall. Then she paused, turned slowly, and walked back.

"Is that you, Scotty? It has been such a long time."

Scott scanned her face without any sign of recognition. "Yes," he said softly as he placed his hand on the door, ready to escape.

"You wouldn't remember me. I had such a crush on you when you were a priest and I was a brand new beehive."

"Cheryl," her husband said softly from his place a dozen yards down the hall. He beckoned with one hand.

"Cheryl Madsen," Scott blurted out as a memory surfaced like a bubble in a lake.

"I'm surprised you remembered me, Scotty. It's Cheryl Barlow now. That's my husband, Cal." She pointed with one hand down the hall. "I'm so sorry about your father." She started down the hallway toward her husband. "It's good to see you again."

Scott nodded his head. He took another deep breath, squeezed his eyes shut, opened them, and walked toward the Relief Society room. Outside the door, he picked up a program. His father's picture stared at him; his chocolate eyes seemed to bore into Scott's. *He's gotten old.* He heard the door behind him open again and the sound of stomping feet as someone shook the snow from his or her shoes. Summoning his courage, he walked into the room. His sister, Jill, stood at the end of the casket; his mother was beside her in a wheelchair. Jill's hair was the color of the falling snow. *Have I gotten that old?* he wondered. Involuntarily, his hand brushed through his hair to the growing bald spot on the crown of his head. Jill was a grown woman. She'd been a teenager when he left.

Scott swallowed hard and joined the line of people moving slowly toward the open coffin, when suddenly his mother's eyes flew open and her jaw dropped. She blinked her eyes, leaned forward in her chair, and beckoned to him. On rubbery knees he moved to her side.

"Scott, you've come," she said with a quavering voice as tears streamed down her face. "I hoped you would. No, I knew you would." She wrapped her fingers around his arms and pulled him down into a hug. He hugged her back awkwardly before standing up.

He looked at his sister. "Hi, sis," he whispered.

Jill gave him a glare that would have ignited a lump of coal. She spoke not a word as her jaw clenched.

I deserve that. His mother pushed him into a spot on her left side. Jill stood on her right. He felt as if he were a prisoner on trial and everyone else in the room was there to condemn him. If only they'd known his father the way he had, they'd understand.

CHAPTER 2

Monday, May 27, 1974

If you want to cry, I'll give you something to cry about!" Randall Simms brushed the dirt off his hands. "Quit your blubbering and tell me what happened."

Scott swiped the back of his hand under his runny nose and wiped it on his pant leg. "Ronny hit me with the ball." Sniffling, he tried to keep from crying. Ron Madsen lived next door.

"Big deal. When are you going to grow up and act like a big boy?" Randall turned back to the bucket of soapy water at his feet, dipped in a sponge, and continued washing the car. Without so much as a glance over his shoulder he said, "You're eight years old, Scott. Start acting like it." With a final swirl, he finished the task, picked up the hose nozzle, and sprayed the suds from the car.

Scott made a wide circle around his father, climbed up the porch steps, and entered the house. His mother was humming to herself as she worked in the kitchen getting the picnic lunch ready for the Memorial Day celebration in the city park. Timidly, he made his way to her side. A dozen slices of bread were lying in a row on the countertop, and his mother had an open jar of mayonnaise in one hand and a knife in the other. "Hi, sweetheart."

Scott struggled to contain the tears. "Hi, Mom."

"What's wrong?" she said as she set the knife down on the counter and sank to her knees.

Scott burst into tears. Between sobs he choked out, "Ronny hit me with the ball." He patted his chest to show her where he'd been struck.

"Let's see." She lifted his shirt and revealed a red spot in the middle of his chest. "I'll bet that hurt," she said gently. "Let me get some ice to put on it."

Scott watched as his mother pulled a dish towel out of a drawer, placed a half dozen ice cubes on it, folded it, and crushed the ice with a wooden mallet that hung above the stove. "Go lie down on the couch," she said, and when Scott complied, she placed the ice pack on his wound.

By then the stinging had almost gone away, and he wasn't sure he needed any further ministration, but it felt good to have someone understand how much it hurt.

He was still lying there when the back door opened and his father stepped into the kitchen. He grabbed a towel and dried his hands. "Car sure was filthy," he said. He spotted Scott lying on the couch in the living room. "What's he doing on the couch with his shoes on?"

"He was hit with a ball. He had a big sore spot on his chest."

"If he'd stayed and helped me wash the car instead of running off, he wouldn't have gotten hurt. Besides, his shoes are going to get the couch dirty. Can't we ever have anything nice around here?" Randall strode into the living room, grabbed Scott's feet, and pulled them off the couch sending him to the floor. The ice pack fell into his lap. His lip started to quiver.

"Now you're going to get ice all over the floor. Get up and throw it in the sink. You weren't hurt that bad." With a shake of his head, Randall walked out the front door and slammed it behind him.

Scott picked up the ice chips, threw them in the sink, and slunk down the hallway to his bedroom.

CHAPTER 3

Scott, I can't believe how distinguished you've become," a woman said as she took his hand in hers. "Welcome home. I'm just sorry it has to be at such a sorrowful time." He nodded his head, but in his heart he thought, *Sorrowful? Hardly, it's a time of relief for me.* He struggled to remember the woman's name.

Apparently seeing the confusion on his face, she added, "It's been such a long time, you probably don't remember me. I'm Pauline Renfrow; I was your Primary teacher a long time ago." Scott nodded his head and tried to smile. Sister Renfrow let go of Scott's hand and reached for his mother's. "Colleen, how are you holding up?"

The next man in line grasped his hand, "I'm Gerald Oscarson and this is my wife, Trudy. I don't believe we've met."

"I'm Scott, the wayward son," he said without further explanation.

A wan smile crossed Gerald's face. "We're so sorry to hear of your dad's passing. He was such a kind man."

You wouldn't think so if you'd been his son. "Thank you." He glanced at the clock on the opposite wall. The viewing was supposed to be over. How come so many people were coming to honor his father?

A half dozen more couples, most of them elderly, passed through the line before Scott glanced at the doorway and did a double take. Richard Newman, his best friend all through high school, stood

8

smiling at him. His dark auburn hair was streaked with gray, but his eyes and the quirky smile on his lips hadn't changed. He winked at Scott from across the room. Scott waited as another dozen couples expressed their condolences before Richard reached out and threw his arms around Scott in a bear hug.

"Scotty, you rascal, where have you been?"

Scott extricated himself. "Around."

"This is Penny, my wife." She extended her hand.

Scott shook her hand while he looked into her eyes. They were the color of wind-swept waves. She smiled at him. "I've heard so much about you," she said. She paused for a split second before continuing with the hint of a smile on her lips, "Most of it good."

While Scott was shaking hands with Penny, the man behind her extended his hand and took Richard's. "President, good to see you."

Scott's eyes skipped to his old friend's. "President?"

"A great stake president," the man said with a nod of his head. "You were an inspiration to us all."

"You?" Scott said.

"Guilty. You know the old story; they look for the most compassionate, loving person in the stake, the one with the best organizational skills, and call her husband as president." He paused before he said softly with a smile, "Thank heaven for repentance."

Scott stood speechless. His mind flitted back to when the two of them had been the town rowdies. It wasn't that they'd done anything terribly wrong, but they still were responsible for a great deal of chaos. Slowly he shook his head.

CHAPTER 4

Friday, October 9, 1981

Scott drove slowly through the parking lot between the football field and the gym. Across the field he could see the scoreboard. They were just beginning the fourth quarter of the game. "We'd better hurry."

Richard Newman nodded his head. "Pull over next to the curb," he said as he grabbed the door handle and eased the door of the pickup truck open. Behind him in the bed of the truck, covered with a tarp, two small pigs snuffled and oinked. Scott stopped the truck, jumped out, and helped Richard lift the canvas off the pigs. An almost overpowering odor assailed their nostrils. There were copious droppings in the bed of the truck.

"Man," Richard said with a shake of his head, "That almost makes my eyes water. We're going to have to wash out the truck before you take it home."

Scott nodded his head. "I'll hit the car wash on the way home." The pigs were racing back and forth frantically in the bed of the truck. Scott climbed up on the bumper and snagged one of them as it tried to escape. He threw his arm under its belly and lifted it out of the truck. The pig squealed and struggled to evade his grasp; a moment later Richard succeeded in subduing the other animal. Quickly, they carried their prey to the door that led into the locker room and awkwardly held onto the struggling pigs while Richard opened the door.

"How did you know it would be unlocked?" Scott asked.

Richard caught the door with his foot and pulled it open all the way. "They always leave it open during the games in case somebody has to get in to get water or ice or something."

On the other side of the locker room was a door that led into the gymnasium itself. Holding onto their squirming charges, the two of them opened the door. Immediately, they let the two pigs loose into the gym before they closed the door, turned, and fled back to the truck.

The two of them high fived as they pulled away. "We'd better hurry home and change if we're coming back to the stomp," Richard said with a chuckle.

Five minutes later, Scott dropped Richard off at his home and hurried to the coin-operated car wash on the old highway. He emptied the coins from his pocket. There was either enough money to wash the truck or pay for the ticket to the stomp. He considered his options and finally decided to wash out the truck at home. A few minutes later he pulled into the driveway, turned on the garden hose, and washed out the bed of the truck. A pungent, aromatic mist engulfed him. He was putting the hose away when the back porch light came on. The door flew open and Scott's father stepped onto the porch.

"What in the world . . ." He swatted the air in front of his nose trying to dissipate the aroma. "Scott! Get in the house! Now!"

Sheepishly, Scott slunk into the kitchen. The odor of pig droppings entered with him.

Randall leaned forward with his hands on the edge of the table. "Would you like to explain yourself?" The anger in his voice could have cut steel. "I thought you and your friend were going to the football game."

"We were," Scott stammered.

"And?" His father's jaw clenched so tightly his lips seemed to be a thin slice across his face.

"Richard sort of had this idea," Scott stammered trying to think of an excuse. Sweat ran down his forehead. His father glowered at him.

"What are the rules?" Randall said with a voice so menacing that Scott expected the air around him to crackle.

Scott bowed his head. "Go straight to the game and come straight home." His voice was barely a whisper.

"So?"

"Richard . . ."

He said no more before his father slammed his hands down on the tabletop. "I'm not asking about Richard. I'm asking what you did."

Scott shook his head, trying to deflect his father's wrath.

"Never mind. Scott, you are such a disappointment to me." He spun around and marched out of the kitchen. "You are grounded for the next month."

Scott almost burst into tears. "Dad, the prom is in two weeks."

"Well, you should have thought about that before you broke the rules. Now quit sniveling and go to your room."

Scott knew it was hopeless to expect any mercy from his father. He crept down the hallway to his bedroom, took one last look over his shoulder, and slammed the door. A moment later his father threw it open. "That just earned you another month of suspension!"

Saturday was spent completely cleaning the pickup truck until it matched his father's expectations. He'd heard nothing else about the stomp and wondered if Richard had gone and what the result of their prank had been.

Sunday morning he left before the rest of the family and made his way to church. Priesthood opening exercises were about to begin. Bishop Gerber was waiting at the door when Scott arrived. "I'm glad you're here early, Scott. I know it's not your turn at the sacrament table, but I just had a call from Brother Newman, and apparently Richard won't be here today. Can you fill in for him?"

Scott shriveled a little. "I guess, Bishop."

"Good. I knew I could count on you." He patted Scott on the shoulder. A few minutes later, priesthood meeting began. Randall walked grimly to a seat near the front of the chapel, clearly avoiding sitting next to his son. It was one of those rare days when he attended church. Opening exercises concluded, and Scott made his way to his quorum meeting. Their advisor began teaching the lesson and was trying to get some participation from the class when the door opened and Bishop Gerber stepped into the room. A cloud of gloom covered his face. He sat down and exhaled loudly.

Priesthood meeting ended, and all of the priests began exiting the room. "Scott, hold on," the bishop said. When all the others had left, the bishop pointed at a chair. "Have a seat." Numbly, Scott sat down. "Your father tells me you might not be worthy to bless the sacrament. What do you have to say to that?"

"Bishop," he struggled for words as a wave of guilt washed over him. "Probably not," he choked out. "Probably not." He sprang to his feet and raced out of the room. Scott left the chapel and wandered around town trying to build up the courage to face his father. He walked past the church in time to see people leaving and then continued roving until he realized he was outside Richard's house. He climbed the porch steps and knocked on the door. Richard's father answered it a minute later.

"Scott, I'm afraid Richard is grounded," he said without preamble. "Oh."

Brother Newman nodded his head slowly. "It seems he was involved in a little prank last night that got out of hand."

Scott was unsure whether Brother Newman knew that he was involved or not. He decided to play dumb. "What happened?"

Brother Newman stared at Scott through his glasses. "Don't you know?" Scott shook his head. "They had to cancel the stomp after the game."

"Why?" Scott was still unsure what Brother Newman knew.

"It took a dozen of us to clean up after two pigs were turned loose in the gym; two pigs that were stolen from Brother Hatch." He shook his head. "Richard finally told me what happened. He has apologized to the principal." He peered into Scott's eyes. "I'm so disappointed in my son." He removed his glasses and wiped tears from his eyes before he replaced them and focused on Scott. "But, I think you know what happened. Or am I wrong?"

Scott shrugged his shoulders. "I'd better get home," he said, avoiding the question. When he arrived home, his father refused to talk with him.

The next day, he and Richard were suspended for three days from school.

CHAPTER 5

Friday, December 18, 2015

You were stake president how long?" Scott managed to say as he tried to forget memories from the past.

"Nine years. I was released nearly eight years ago. It's a strong stake; even *I* wasn't able to ruin it." He clapped Scott on the shoulder. "What about you?"

"Not much to say," Scott mumbled.

Richard raised an eyebrow and glanced at his watch. "When did you get here? Have you had dinner yet? It's pretty late."

Scott shook his head. "No. I drove straight here, but I need to spend time with Mom."

"Straight from where? Where are you living now? I lost track of you thirty years ago."

"Keokuk, Iowa."

"Keokuk? Where's that?"

"East side of the state—on the banks of the Mississippi."

Penny glanced at the people behind them. "Honey, I'm sure Scott wants to spend time with his family. We're holding up the line."

"How long will you be in town?" Richard asked.

"I'm not sure. A day or two. The funeral's tomorrow. Well, of course you knew that."

"Well, carve out some time so we can catch up on old times. Okay?"

Scott couldn't think of a way to avoid it without seeming rude, so he shrugged his shoulders. "Okay."

Newman reached into the inside pocket of his coat, retrieved a card, and handed it to Scott. "Call me. Maybe we could meet at Swenson's, just like old times."

Scott glanced at the card before slipping it into his pocket—*Dr. Richard Newman, MD.* "Sure."

Richard gave him a wink as he grasped Colleen's hand. "Mixed emotions?" he said. Colleen nodded her head.

Scott looked at his sister. She stared back him. Her lips were pressed so tightly together they formed a hard white line across her face. She gave a slight bob of her head encouraging him to keep the line moving. He gave a small nod of his head.

Scott took a deep breath as the next person in line extended his hand, "We're the Sandovals," he said, waiting for Scott to identify himself.

"I'm Scott, the black sheep in the family," he said with the wisp of a smile.

Brother Sandoval's eyebrows shot up. "I didn't know Brother Simms had a son," he exclaimed.

Scott swallowed. "Well, I haven't been around for quite some time."

Scott's mother reached up from her wheelchair. "Oh, Kurt and Naomi, thank you for coming. It's been such a long time since I saw you." She looked up at her son. "The Sandovals bought the Harrington home about twenty years ago."

"Twenty-two," Naomi said.

"Then they moved to . . . I've forgotten where. My mind isn't as sharp as it used to be. They say it comes with age, but I think it goes with age."

"We moved to Mesa," Naomi said gently. "My husband was transferred."

"Certainly you didn't come all this way for Randall's funeral."

Kurt Sandoval patted the back of her hand, "You know we would have anyway, but it turned out we were in Provo picking up our daughter, Melissa, from BYU."

"Well, it's so good of you to think of us at a time like this."

Sister Sandoval turned back to Scott. "Your father was such a wonderful man. You must miss him."

Scott bit back the bitter retort that came to mind. Instead he said, "How did you know my father?"

"Oh, it's a long story; he extended a hand when we moved into the ward." She smiled and followed her husband down the line past the casket.

Scott's mother smiled at him. "Their daughter is quite the musician. She's pretty smart, too. I believe she was awarded a full scholarship at the Y." She reached up and patted Scott's hand. "Just like you."

CHAPTER 6

Thursday, June 9, 1983

Inside Abravanel Hall, nearly every seat was filled. A hundred conversations were being carried on in hushed voices. People fanned themselves with the programs that had been handed out at the door.

Outside, Mrs. Reese and Mr. Briscoe were checking out the graduates' caps and gowns and arranging them in proper order in preparation for the march into the hall.

Mrs. Reese led Sally Silvester to her place in front of Scott. She had a small plastic trash bucket in her hand. "Gum, Sally," Mrs. Reese said as she held up the container. Sally rolled her eyes before she removed a wad from her mouth and dropped it in the bucket.

Mrs. Reese looked over Sally's shoulder into Scott's eyes. "Scott, I'm so glad we were able to get you that full-ride scholarship to BYU."

"Couldn't have done it without your help," he said with a smile.

"Nonsense. With your grades and how well you did on the ACT, you were a shoe-in. You could have had your pick. All of the colleges in the state wanted you."

Scott blushed. "Thanks." The pig incident was far behind him, thankfully, and he'd become a serious student.

"So what are your plans?"

Scott hesitated a moment. "Dad wants me to go into medicine," he said with a shrug of his shoulders.

"You'd make a great doctor," Mrs. Reese said with a nod of her head.

"Thanks. Of course, Dad wants me to go on a mission first."

"Well, you'll be a great missionary."

"I guess."

"Do I detect a little hesitancy on your part?"

Scott shrugged his shoulders. "Maybe. I'm not sure I want to be . . ."

Suddenly, Mrs. Reese stiffened. "Roger, I know you'd like to be next to Melissa, but you need to line up alphabetically." She turned back to Scott. "Excuse me." She walked purposefully to where Roger Bangerter was trying to line up out of order. She led him to the right spot in the line. As if on cue, the doors opened and the sounds of "Pomp and Circumstances" greeted the waiting seniors. "Good luck," Mrs. Reese said to Scott as he entered the hall.

They marched down the aisle and seated themselves on risers on the stage. Scott searched the crowd before him and finally located his mother, father, and sister sitting in the first balcony. The senior class president, John Collins, walked to the microphone, welcomed the audience, and announced that the concert choir would sing the opening song, "May the Road Rise to Meet You."

When the number was finished, John stepped to the podium again. "We will now hear from our valedictorian, Scott Simms."

Scott had struggled with his talk ever since he'd been notified he'd be speaking. He wanted to say something that would be remembered, but most of all he didn't want to embarrass himself or his family. He forced a smile in his family's direction as he made his way to the podium. And he hoped to make a point.

"Parents, administration, faculty, and fellow graduates," he began. "Today we stand on the threshold of the rest of our lives. For the last three years the faculty and administration have watched over us and guided us; but tonight we embark on our own journeys. For some there will be opportunities that lead to great wealth and fame.

For some there will be trials. For all of us there will be great learning experiences.

"Our parents have tried to direct us down paths that will guarantee success; however, there are no guarantees. Some of us will fail. But it is not in failing that there is defeat, it is only if we do not rise and try again. Let me tell you a story that might give you a reason to think about your own goals and aspirations.

"There was once an old stonecutter named David. All day long he sat in his small shop and with a hammer and chisel created headstones for the people of his town. One day, a general came through the town leading a hundred men. The general sat atop a snow-white stallion that snorted and tossed its head.

"'Oh,' said David, 'What I would give to be that general, for he is mightier than I!'

"Suddenly a small voice whispered in his ear, 'David, if you would be that general, be that general.' And with a small clap of thunder, David found himself in the saddle of the stallion wearing armament and carrying a sword. He was excited and proud and very happy.

"David led his hundred troops out of the town and into the surrounding countryside. After a few hours, the troops began to grumble because of the heat of the sun and the lack of water.

"David wiped the sweat from his brow, shaded his eyes, and looked toward the sun. 'Oh, how I wish I were the sun, for he is mightier than I!' Again the voice whispered, 'David, if you would be the sun, be the sun.'

"Again there was a clap of thunder and David found himself in the sky shining down on the world. He was very happy.

"He watched as all the people who walked in the sunlight removed their cloaks and wiped the sweat from their faces; and he was overjoyed—until a little cloud scudded between him and the men on the road. David burned down with all his might on the cloud, but the harder he focused, the bigger the cloud became.

"'Oh,' he said, 'I wish I were that cloud, for he is mightier than I.'

"Again the voice came, this time a little weary, and said, 'David, if you would be the cloud, be the cloud.'

"And with a clap of thunder, David found himself floating in the sky, raining on the folks below. He watched them run for cover and try to keep the water from their eyes. He was very happy—until one day he saw a huge boulder on the side of the hill, and he decided he would wash away the earth surrounding it until it fell into the valley. He poured rain upon the rock with all the wrath he could muster, but still it remained in place. Lightning and thunder flashed and rolled across the hillside—but still the boulder resisted the downpour.

"'Oh, I wish I were that boulder, for it is mightier than I.'

"'David, if you would be the boulder, be the boulder,' the weary voice whispered. And with a final clap of thunder, David found himself a monolith of stone on the hillside. Travelers approached on the path and detoured around him; and he was very happy.

"Then an old stonecutter made his way up the path, placed his steel chisel against the base of the rock, and began to hammer. David found himself beginning to lose his footing. The hammer and chisel flaked away bits of his base chip by chip. He could tell he would soon fall over.

"'Oh, I wish I were a stonecutter,' David said in desperation, 'for surely he is mightier than I.'

"And for the last time, the voice whispered, 'Then David, be a stonecutter, for that is what you were meant to be.'"

Scott looked up from his notes at his parents in the first balcony and said with determination, "May we all discover and become what we were meant to be regardless of what others might want us to be." He turned and returned to his seat. The audience applauded enthusiastically.

The rest of the program went as outlined and finally the graduates walked across the stage to receive their diplomas. The superintendent, a member of the school board, and the principal were standing in a line shaking hands with each graduate. As the principal shook Scott's hand he said, "Great speech. From all I've heard from your father, I think I know what you're going to be." Scott looked at his father in the balcony before he nodded his head.

CHAPTER 7

A dozen more couples arrived and visited briefly with the family before the viewing ended.

Scott took his mother's hand in his, "I guess I'll be going."

"Going? Where?"

"I've rented a motel room," he said.

His mother looked shocked. "Nonsense. Cancel it; you'll come home with me."

"Mother," Jill spat, "Let him go to his motel."

"Jill, Jill, don't be silly. I have plenty of room, and we need to catch up on a lot of history."

Jill stared at Scott with an anthracitic stare. "If you insist." She grabbed the handles of the wheelchair and pushed her mother out the door. Over her shoulder she said, "I suppose you can find the way. Some things haven't changed that much in thirty years." Numbly, Scott nodded his head.

He took one last look at his father in the casket. He was so much older than Scott remembered. "Well thirty-two years will do that, I suppose," he said to himself. The funeral directors were closing the casket and a member of the bishopric was turning out the lights.

Scott climbed into the cab of his truck, deciding whether to drive to his mother's home or not. His sister certainly didn't want to welcome him. Still, he owed it to his mother. She had grown so old and frail—why didn't he realize that she'd age? He certainly had.

The snowflakes had increased in intensity, and his windshield was covered. He started the truck, turned on the wipers, and waited for the heater to defrost the windows. With a sigh, he drove the six blocks from the chapel to his mother's house, pulled into the driveway, and turned off the ignition. All of the houses on the street had Christmas lights hanging from the eaves. A kaleidoscope of colors lit up the blanket of snow in the front yards and dressed the flakes in holiday hues.

Scott opened the door of the truck and stepped into the snow. *I should have worn my parka.* Tentatively, he crossed the front yard and climbed the steps to the porch. A Christmas tree stood in the front window, the star on top blinking on and off. Scott stopped at the door and debated whether he should ring the bell or just walk in.

Before he could decide, the door opened. His mother sat in her wheelchair with her arms spread wide. "Oh, Scott, it's so good to see you. Welcome home." Awkwardly, he bent down and hugged his mother again. He struggled to find something to say, but gave up and followed her into the living room. Memories flooded back as he looked around.

"You've painted," he said.

"Several times," his mother answered. She pointed at the couch, "Sit, sit."

Scott lowered himself onto the floral brocade couch. It was very different from the one he remembered from his youth. "It looks nice." He felt a strange mixture of relief and anxiety. "And you have a grand piano."

"Thank you. It's a baby grand. Jill is quite an accomplished pianist." She wheeled herself until she was in front of him. "You've made my holiday," she said.

Scott fiddled with his thumbs while he tried to think of something to say. At last he ventured, "I'm sorry it took his death to bring me home."

Tears brimmed in his mother's eyes. "If you'd have come sooner, he might not have recognized you anyway."

"Alzheimer's?"

She nodded her head, swallowed, and stared past Scott at the ceiling. "It started when he was seventy-five and just got worse." She pulled a dainty lace handkerchief from the cuff of her blouse and dabbed at the tears. "His mind just seemed to slip away, day after day."

"I understand," Scott replied with a shrug of his shoulders. "It couldn't have been easy." He struggled to find something to say. "Where's Jill?"

"She went home after dropping me off."

"From what she said, I thought she was living with you."

"She and Dan bought the old Page home."

"Dan?"

"Her husband, Dan Palmer. You wouldn't have known him; he moved here with his family the year after . . . after you left."

"Oh." Scott shook his head, "I didn't know she'd married. I guess I have a lot to catch up on. Where was her husband at the viewing?"

His mother lowered her head and fought back tears. "He died nearly ten years ago. Both of her children were married and gone."

"I'm sorry. How did he die?"

"He had a ruptured appendix while he had the scouts up in the Uintah Mountains." She sighed. "They tried to save him, but the infection had spread . . . let's not talk about it."

"Okay. Tell me about Jill's children—she has two?"

"Jim and Jenny. Jim works with computers. I don't really understand what he does. He and his wife, Meg, live in Seattle with their kids. Jenny and her husband, Gordon, live in Sacramento—he works for the State of California."

"Are they coming for the funeral? Do you see them often?"

"More often than I've seen you." She shook her head. "I'm sorry, I didn't mean to sound bitter."

"That's all right, I deserved it."

"But to answer your question, they're here. They drove in this afternoon. They came to the viewing, but they were so tired I sent them home, just before you arrived. I thought things were wrapping up. I should have known it would take longer for all our friends to pay their respects."

He looked at the Christmas tree. Many of the ornaments were the same as the ones he'd put on the tree when he was a child growing up. One of them caught his eye, and he rose to his feet and walked to the tree. A small, red plastic jewel was imbedded in a circle of baked clay. He reached out and cradled it in the palm of his hand, then turned it over and saw his name scribbled with a toothpick.

"First grade," his mother said softly. "You brought it home from school and we hung it on the tree."

"I can't believe you still have it." He removed it from the tree and examined it more closely.

His mother straightened herself in her chair before she spoke. "It was one of the things we had to remember you by." There was no chastisement in her voice, only wistfulness.

Scott returned to the couch, sat down, and hung his hands between his knees. "I was such a disappointment." The ornament hung from one finger.

"Oh, Scott, you were never a disappointment."

"Maybe not to you, but I never satisfied . . . my father." He tried to choke out "Dad," but it stuck in his throat like a dry burr.

After a quiet pause his mother said, "Why do you feel that way?"

"Because I never did anything that was good enough for him." He looked down at the Christmas decoration dangling from his finger. "He told me this ornament was ugly. He was embarrassed to have it on the tree." He shook his head. "Even when I took first place it wasn't good enough." He was surprised at how much anger still burned in his chest.

Chapter 8

Thursday, August 9, 1973

Scott pounded his right hand into this first baseman's mitt while he took two steps toward second base. His team, the Eagles, was ahead five to four in the last inning. Their biggest rivals, the Blue Devils, had two men on base with two outs, and their strongest batter was up. Richard Newman, the pitcher, threw the ball with all the might his eight-year-old arm could muster. The batter fouled the pitch—no balls, one strike. The catcher lobbed the ball back to Richard, who scraped his well-worn tennis shoe on the mound before winding up and throwing the next pitch—outside and low—one ball, one strike.

Scott crouched down with his hands on his knees as Richard wound up for the next pitch. The batter lifted the bat off his shoulder as the ball was delivered and with a mighty swing, sent the ball bouncing down the first base line. Scott reacted quickly and as the ball reached him, he grabbed it with his mitt and stomped onto first base. Third out! Game won! The Eagles had taken the championship!

The team raced to the pitcher's mound jumping and screaming. Richard pounded Scott on the shoulder. "Way to go!" he screamed. It took a few minutes until the coaches could get the two teams to line up and congratulate each other before the short awards ceremony. Coach Hall lifted the trophy above his head in triumph while the boys hung their medals around their necks.

Mrs. Hall had brought bags of Spudnuts and a cooler full of root beer. The celebration went on for half an hour or so before parents became impatient and started taking the boys home.

Scott climbed into the back seat of their three-year-old Ford Falcon with his six-year-old sister, Jill. His dad and mom slid into the front seat. "Roll down the windows," his father said. "It's hot in here. You'd think they'd play when it's cooler." Obediently, Scott rolled down the window on his side of the car before reaching across Jill to roll down her window.

"You played really well," his mother said.

Scott slipped the red, white, and blue ribbon over his head and inspected the small gold medal. "Want to see?" he asked his mother.

She reached over the seat and took it in her hand. "It's beautiful," she exclaimed. She handed it back to Scott and said, "And all because you were able to make that last out."

"Well, if you'd played better the first three innings you'd have been so far ahead they wouldn't have had to rely on you making that play. After all, you struck out twice." Scott's father shook his head.

"Oh, Randall, don't be so negative," Colleen said with a tight smile.

"I'm just saying it the way it is," Randall answered with a growl. "And you'd think they'd give these kids a bigger medal for taking first place. That one's hardly worth looking at."

Scott looked at the medal in his hand. It wasn't very big. When they reached home he went into his bedroom and dropped the medal in the bottom of his sock drawer.

A few minutes later the telephone rang. "Scott, it's for you," his mother called from the kitchen. Scott walked slowly to the phone.

"Hello."

"Hey, Scotty, guess what?" Richard Newman said.

"What?" Scott answered.

"My dad's taking us to Yankee Lunch to celebrate!"

"Wow!"

"What are you guys doing?"

Scott looked across the kitchen to where his mother was heating soup on the stove. "Not much," Scott said, trying to sound positive. He realized that his family had gone out to dinner only once in his lifetime. They never celebrated anything.

CHAPTER 9

Friday, December 18, 2015

Scott shook his head and returned to the present. "I wish I'd been a better son."

"I couldn't have asked for anyone better," she said simply.

Scott shook his head. "My father could have."

They sat in silence for a few minutes while the blinking star on the Christmas tree kept time to his heartbeat. "Scott, let me tell you something about your father."

"If you need to."

"I think I do; I think it will help you understand him a little better." She paused, wiped her mouth with a tissue, then began. "Your father was a very insecure man."

Scott laughed. "My father? You've got to be kidding. He took charge of everything."

"Yes, he did, because he had to demonstrate that he was better than everyone else he was working with."

"Oh, really?" Scott shook his head in disbelief.

"When I first met his family, when we were dating, I began to understand your father. I don't wish to speak ill of the dead, but his father and mother were unsmiling, sour people. They gave none of their children any praise or love. They were expected to do their chores and shut up." Her voice had risen in intensity. "Randall was never told he was worth anything. I think he decided that he'd prove his parents wrong—although I'm not sure he ever realized it consciously. So, every time he was involved in a project, he had to make sure it was done better than anyone else had done it before."

"I'm not sure I understand."

"He needed the praise. He needed to feel superior."

Scott's forehead knitted. "I still don't understand."

"Well, for example, the ward breakfast."

"Every Fourth of July," he said as a memory stirred.

"You remember. Well, one year your father was put on the committee . . . I think the bishop was trying to activate him. It was the year after you left." She raised an eyebrow waiting for Scott to speak. He just sat on the sofa wringing his hands.

"What happened?" he finally asked.

"Scott, you might not remember, but for twenty years we always had scrambled eggs, pancakes, and bacon at the breakfast."

Scott nodded his head. "I think I remember that."

"Well, your father tried to convince them to change the menu."

Scott's forehead wrinkled. "And how did that go over?"

"Unfortunately, there were some feelings hurt. As you can expect, your father kind of dominated the committee."

"I can understand that. It probably made more work for everyone."

Colleen nodded her head toward her son. "It did, and he ended up having to pay for some of it out of his own pocket rather than admit they'd gone over budget." She paused. "Do you understand why?"

Scott looked even more confused. "Not really."

"Because in his mind it was better than the years before, and your father would prove he was superior—because he felt so inferior."

"That's crazy."

"Maybe, but it carried over into everything he did, because no matter how well he did something, he could see where it could be improved."

"Even stuff he'd done?"

She nodded her head. "Especially things he'd done." She paused and looked at her clenched hands. After a moment, she shifted uncomfortably. "There was a time, early in our marriage, when things weren't going very smoothly between us."

"I can understand why." Scott interlaced his fingers and rested them on his knee. "Mom, I'm not sure why you put up with him."

Tears formed in Colleen's eyes. "Oh, Scott, because I loved him. And because I could see how deep inside he was such a good man." She took a deep breath. "It has been so hard to see him go downhill so quickly."

"I'm sorry, Mom. That was insensitive of me." Scott shook his head slowly and waited for his mother to regain her composure.

"Scott, I hope you'll keep this just between the two of us."

"Of course."

Colleen took a deep breath and exhaled slowly. "I spoke to our bishop and he helped me meet with a counselor."

"Just you?"

"Your father refused to go." She paused and tried to compose herself. "I've never told anyone else this before, Scott." She lapsed into silence.

A moment passed before he said, "You don't have to tell me, if you're uncomfortable."

"It's about time I told someone, and you're the one who needs to hear it."

"I understand," he said softly.

Colleen steeled herself before she continued. "Let me tell you about the first meeting I had with the counselor."

CHAPTER 10

Monday, May 15, 1967

olleen Simms stood in the hallway outside Dr. Mower's office summoning enough courage to open the door. Bishop Lemon had made the arrangements, but she still was unsure she was doing the right thing. She took a deep breath and pushed the door open.

The office was decorated in tasteful shades of pale blue with navy blue accents. Three couches formed a U around an oriental rug. The receptionist smiled at her as Colleen stood rooted to a spot just inside the door.

"Mrs. Simms?" the woman asked.

Colleen nodded her head and finally forced her feet to move her to the counter. "Yes," she said timidly.

"Dr. Mower is just finishing up with another patient. Please have a seat and he'll be with you shortly."

"Thank you."

"While you're waiting, would you mind filling out these forms?" The receptionist handed her a clipboard with a few sheets of paper.

Colleen took them and made her way to one of the couches. It took several minutes to answer all the questions and just as she finished with them, the door next to the receptionist opened; Dr. Mower walked to her and extended his hand.

"Mrs. Simms, please." He helped her to her feet and led her down a short hallway to his office. He was quite tall and had a shock of unruly dark brown hair with silver strands at the temples. He gave her a warm smile as he gestured toward a leather recliner that sat in one corner of the room. "Comfortable?" he asked.

Colleen answered that she was.

Dr. Mower seated himself behind his desk. "Now, if I'm not mistaken, you're nervous and a little embarrassed about being here." He smiled.

"I guess so," Colleen said.

"Well, let me make two things crystal clear to you before we go any further. First, nothing that is discussed in this office will go any farther. It is completely confidential. Second, you are amazingly brave for seeking help. Most people just try to ignore problems in hope that they'll go away." He shrugged his shoulders. "Sometimes they do, but usually they just fester until some sort of explosion occurs."

Colleen nodded her head.

"So, having said that, why don't you tell me about yourself?"

Colleen clenched her fists tightly and then tried to relax them. "I really don't know where to begin," she said in a voice barely above a whisper.

Dr. Mower rested his hands on the edge of his desk while he waited patiently. "Then let me guess at a few things." He waited for her to nod her head. "I suspect your husband is doing some things that really annoy you. Am I right?" Colleen nodded her head again. "Why don't you tell me just one thing that is bothering you?"

She sat silently for a few moments while Dr. Mower smiled at her and waited as if he had all the time in the world. Finally she said, "This is kind of strange." He raised an eyebrow. "I mean, my husband never listens to me."

"He doesn't listen to what you have to say."

"He interrupts me if I try to say something."

Dr. Mower nodded his head.

Colleen said, "He just has to be in charge all the time."

Dr. Mower made a note on the pad in front of him. "He wants to have you do things his way."

Colleen nodded her head again. "Dr. Mower, I try to do what he wants, but it's never good enough."

He made another note. "Nothing you ever do meets his standards."

"Oh, it's not just me. He's just not satisfied with anything. He can see the negative in everything. It's like he expects it."

"Can you give me an example?"

Colleen thought for a moment. "Well, when he calls someone on the phone, while it's ringing he'll say, 'They're probably not home.'"

Dr. Mower chuckled. "But when they answer, is he surprised?"

"I don't know, honestly."

"Anything else?"

Colleen gathered her thoughts. "It seems like he thinks everyone is trying to cheat him."

"In what way?"

"He says everybody he works with is stupid. Almost every night he tells me about the things all of his coworkers do that are wrong, and that his boss doesn't appreciate him and isn't living up to the agreements they made when Randall went to work for him." Once she began to speak, the words seemed to cascade from her mouth.

Dr. Mower jotted a few notes on the pad in front of him. "How does he treat you? You indicated nothing you did ever pleased him."

Again there was a pause. "He can find fault with anything."

Dr. Mower rubbed his chin. "I'm going to ask you a very direct question." Colleen waited and then nodded her head. "Do you want your marriage to work?"

"Of course."

Dr. Mower smiled at her. "Then the next time you come I'm going to teach you a game. It won't be easy, but it might be very helpful. I'm going to take some time going over these notes and by the time we meet again, I think I might be able to offer you some help. Okay?" He stood up, walked to the recliner she was sitting in, and helped her to her feet. "Can we meet next Monday at the same time?"

Colleen nodded her head as Dr. Mower let her out a side door into the hallway.

CHAPTER 11

Friday, December 18, 2015

I went back to see Dr. Mower, and he helped me see how your father's insecurity ruled his life. Much of it went back to the relationship, or the lack of one, that he'd had with his father and mother. He asked again if I really wanted to continue with our marriage. Of course I said I did; after all, you were nearly two years old."

"So you put up with his abuse because of me?"

"Oh, no, Scott. It was because I loved your father." She wiped her eyes with her handkerchief. "Anyway, Dr. Mower helped me make a game out of it."

"What kind of game?" Scott said as his eyebrows knitted.

"Well, whatever the situation, your father always looked for something to criticize or comment on. For example, we never entered the house without him saying, 'It's cold in here,' or, 'It's hot in here.' It didn't matter what the thermometer said, your father just had to make a comment."

"So what was the game?"

"It was pretty simple. Knowing your father would try to find fault, I tried to think what your father would say before he said it."

"Really? That must have been weird."

"Not really; it was actually kind of fun. And over time I got pretty good at it." A smile crossed her lips. "I'd fix a roast for dinner and I'd think, *What can Randall find wrong with dinner? Will he think it's too hot? Too cold? Too rare? Too well-done?* And he'd sit down at the table, look at me and say, 'I thought we were having chicken.'"

Scott looked confused. "But you hadn't thought of that."

"Nope, so I'd add it to my list of things for the next time I fixed dinner."

"And you did this for how many years?"

"Well, we were married for fifty-two years, but I only had to play the game for about twenty of them."

"Why?"

Colleen's eyes filled with tears. "That's another story, Scott. A wonderful story. I need to explain it to you, but it might take some time. Maybe tomorrow."

"Okay."

"But sufficient to say, in the twenty years I played the game, your father never ceased to surprise me."

"In what way?"

She cocked her head and a smile crossed her lips. "One night in the early spring, we went to Temple Square to hear the Mormon Tabernacle Choir rehearse.

"When he reached the Tabernacle your father said, 'I don't know why they don't start at seven o'clock.'

"I answered, 'That's their rehearsal time.' I figured that's what he'd say—I hit that one right on the head.

"The choir members were finding their seats and perusing the music they'd be rehearsing that night when Richard P. Condie, the director, walked through one of the portals and took his place in front of the choir. Immediately, the conversations among choir members ended. He nodded at Brother Roy Darley, who was seated at the organ.

"'Let's begin with 'A Mighty Fortress Is Our God,' Brother Condie said. There was a momentary rustling as the choir members found the appropriate music in their folders. Brother Condie raised his baton and the choir began to sing.

"Between numbers your father leaned over to me and said in a whisper, 'Why do you think they aren't wearing their costumes?'

"'It's just a rehearsal,' I told him. Bingo!

"For two hours we listened to the world famous choir prepare for their Sunday program and then the rehearsal was over. We stood up from the wooden bench on which we'd been sitting and made our way to the door. As we walked out of the building, I played the game and tried to think what Randall would say.

"Your father seemed deep in thought and then he said, 'If they'd dim the lights, it would make the choir sound better.' I nearly laughed out loud because that thought had never entered my mind."

Scott looked puzzled. "But dimming the lights wouldn't affect the sound at all."

"I know that."

"Then why did he say that? I still don't understand."

"Because he wanted to be seen without a fault and he knew he had many. So he found faults in everybody else, trying to make himself look superior."

Scott shook his head. "That sort of makes sense, I guess."

"Of course, that was before the big change came."

"Big change?"

His mother nodded her head. "Oh, yes. You wouldn't believe what happened. As I said, tomorrow we'll talk about that." She smiled enigmatically. "But enough about your father; where did you go? Where have you been? Why did you leave?"

"It's a long story," he said with a sigh.

"We have time," his mother said gently.

Scott took a deep breath. "Well, first I went to California."

"Oh?" she said quizzically. "Who did you know there? "

"No one, really. I went to the bus station and the first bus that was leaving went to San Jose."

CHAPTER 12

Saturday, June 11, 1983

Scott sat on the bus bench and counted the bills he held in his hand. He had $280 left from the money he'd earned working at Bear's Drive Inn his senior year. He sighed. It wasn't much, but enough to get him away from home. Resolutely, he stood, picked up his bag, and walked to the ticket window. "When's the next bus leaving?"

"We have one leaving in twenty minutes for San Jose, California."

"How much is the fare?"

"Thirty-two dollars," the ticket seller replied. "There are two transfers and the trip takes just over nineteen hours."

"I'll take a ticket," Scott said.

Twenty minutes later he boarded the bus, put his bag in the overhead shelf, and settled back into his seat. The bus was less than half full. His emotions swung between anger and regret, but as the bus pulled out of the depot, he closed his eyes and tried to think what the future held for him. By the time they made their first stop in Wendover, he was kicking himself for leaving home and almost got off the bus and made his way back to Salt Lake; but after a moment's reflection he steeled his determination, settled back in his seat, and stared out the window as they made their way across Nevada.

When they passed through Battle Mountain, Scott began wondering what his family would do when he didn't return home. *Mom will cry, but Dad will try to hunt me down.* The realization hit him like a ton of bricks. If he was really going to escape from his father's wrath, he needed to disappear. He looked at his bus ticket. There was a transfer point in Sacramento. It took just a second before Scott realized that if he got off the bus there and didn't return to his seat, it probably wouldn't be noticed.

By the time they reached Reno and then began their climb over Donner Pass, Scott had formulated a plan. He knew his father would be searching for him to drag him home and make him do what his father wanted. He'd get off the bus in Sacramento, change his name, and find work. Satisfied, he sank back in his seat and watched the changing scenery outside the bus window.

Since he had just his small duffle bag, it was easy to walk away from the bus in the Sacramento terminal. He threw his bag over his shoulder and walked out onto L Street. To his left he could see the dome of the state capitol building; he turned toward it and walked the two blocks to 10th Street. He was fascinated by the palm trees that lined the walk, and he gawked at them as he made his way toward the capitol steps. At length he found a stone bench and sat down. The sun was setting behind him and again he wondered whether he was doing the right thing or not. While he sat pondering, a man approached him. He was fairly short and heavily built with a blue bandana covering his head. He wore a leather jacket even though it was a warm day.

The man stopped. "Buddy, you know how I can find Sutter's Fort? It's supposed to be somewhere around here." He looked around furtively as if he was trying to discover if anyone else was around.

Scott shrugged his shoulders. "Sorry, I just got into town myself." He felt vaguely uncomfortable about his situation, so he stood and started walking away from the man down 10th Street. The man followed him a few steps before a young couple rounded the corner. Quickly, he turned around and walked away. *That was weird,* Scott thought. Scott continued wandering down the street without any specific destination in mind. Nearly an hour later he found himself atop a small hill at the entrance to the city cemetery. Although the sun had set, there was still enough light to read the names on the tombstones.

Many of them were large upright stones. He began walking slowly through the grounds reading the names and dates on them. As he turned a corner, he stopped by a grave that apparently had been recently filled; the grass on top showed signs of having been removed and replaced. A shiny, unweathered headstone marked the spot.

"Craig Spillman," Scott read out loud. "May 3, 1966, through April 2, 1983." *Just about my age. I wonder how he died?* His thoughts flew back to his parents. *At least someone cared enough about him to . . . No! That's unfair. My mother cares.* Anger built up in his chest. *But my father wouldn't worry at all. He's probably glad I'm gone. One less thing he has to worry about.* Scott shook his head. *But he'll still try to find me and force me to do what he wants.*

Suddenly a thought entered Scott's mind. *I can become Craig Spillman.* He searched in his duffle for a paper and pencil and wrote down the information from the head stone. Just to the right of Craig Spillman's grave was another larger head stone—*Justin Spillman, August 6, 1937–November 9, 1981.* To the side was inscribed *Mary Lois Spillman, September 19, 1938.* There was no death date. *Probably his parents,* Scott thought. He wrote down that information as well. It had grown dark enough he was having trouble seeing the words on the stones.

He wandered back through town until he found a shabby motel. Twelve dollars later he had a place to sleep for the night. He awoke the next morning and asked the desk clerk how to get to the Department of Health. Half an hour later he stepped off the bus and entered the building. A clerk stepped to the counter and asked if she could help.

"I need to get a birth certificate to handle some insurance questions for my brother who just passed away." He tried to look distraught.

"I'm so sorry," the woman said. "What was his name?"

"Craig Spillman."

"And his date of birth?"

"May 3, 1966," Scott said without a pause.

"Parents' names?"

"Justin and Mary Lois Spillman."

"Please take a seat," she said, indicating a wooden bench. "This will take just a few minutes."

Scott seated himself. The lies had come so easily. As he sat there, his palms began to sweat. After ten minutes, he was so nervous he nearly leapt to his feet and ran out of the building, but just at that moment the clerk returned.

"Here you are," she said with a smile. "That will be five dollars. Do you need a death certificate as well?"

Scott shook his head as he dug a five-dollar bill out of his wallet and handed it to the woman. She handed him a white envelope.

"Do you need a receipt?"

Scott shook his head. "No. Thank you." He took a deep breath to calm himself before he turned and walked away from the counter.

"I'm sorry for your loss," the clerk said as he walked out the door. Scott looked back over his shoulder and nodded at her.

Half an hour later he presented the birth certificate at the Social Security office and applied for a Social Security number and card. Craig Spillman was ready to find a job.

CHAPTER 13

Friday, December 18, 2015

What did you do when you got to San Jose?"

Scott rubbed his hands together between his knees. "Actually I didn't go all the way to San Jose. I decided to stay in Sacramento."

"Why?" Colleen asked.

Scott shrugged his shoulders. "I don't know. I was trying to hide."

"Hide from whom?"

Scott swallowed. "Dad."

Silence settled over the room, suffocating the conversation. The minutes ticked by until Colleen said softly, "I see." She settled back in her wheelchair wondering whether to probe about what exactly had happened to create a big enough schism between Scott and Randall to send him away. After another pause she said, "So what did you do in Sacramento?"

"I went to work at a McDonald's. It was just like Bear's, only a little more organized. Anyway, I'd told them I had experience and they hired me on the spot."

"Where did you stay?"

"Well, one of the other workers, a guy named Juan, was looking for a roommate. I moved in with him."

Silence fell again. "Then what happened?"

"Like I said, it's a long story."

"We have time."

"Mom, I'm really kind of tired. Maybe we could leave this until tomorrow."

Colleen slid a little lower in her chair. "Then we can share two stories. Could you wheel me to my bedroom?"

"Sure." He pushed the wheelchair down the hallway to her bedroom and helped her get out of the chair and into bed. "How long have you been in the chair?"

"Oh, about eight weeks. I broke my hip; slipped off the curb. I go to rehab every day. I ought to be back on my feet within a week."

Scott nodded his head. "So it isn't permanent?"

"No, just a minor setback. I'll be fine."

"Where do you want me to sleep?"

"Your bedroom," she said simply. "Good night. It's wonderful to have you home. I've prayed about you for years."

Scott walked the few steps to his old bedroom door. When he pushed it open, he found it unchanged from when he last slept there, thirty-two years before. The same quilt lay on the bed, and the trophies he'd won were lined up on the shelf above the table he'd used as a desk. The room was spotless; it was clear it had been dusted and cleaned regularly. It was clear someone cared. A surge of melancholy hit him. He made his way back to his truck and retrieved the small suitcase he'd brought with him. Once he was back in the house he locked the door, turned off the Christmas lights, and walked softly down the hallway to his room. He undressed, drew back the covers, and slipped into sheets that had awaited him for three decades.

Even though he'd driven for over eighteen hours, he found it hard to fall asleep. He was bone weary, but his mind kept slipping back into the past. He mulled over what his mother had said—no doubt it was painful for her to reveal what she'd told him—and tried to make sense of how his father had treated him as a boy. What big change had occurred? And why?

He finally drifted off into a troubled sleep, struggling to remember one event—any event—in his life that made his father happy. All he could seem to remember was constant criticism.

CHAPTER 14

Saturday, April 16, 1983

Scott, get over here right now!" his father yelled at him from the back porch.

Scott closed the garage door and walked across the patio to where his father stood fuming. "What?" He tried to keep his voice neutral.

Randall tapped the edge of an envelope on the railing. "Utah State University? Really?"

"They have a great engineering program," Scott blurted out.

"So what? You're going to be a doctor, not an engineer."

Scott felt the anger swell in his chest. "Did you open my mail?"

His father shook his head. "Were you trying to hide this from me?"

Scott took a deep breath. "My counselor said I should investigate every option."

"You have a full-ride scholarship to BYU. Once you finish your bachelor's there, you'll be able to choose any medical school you want." He slapped the envelope against his palm. "This is just a bunch of nonsense." Without another word, he spun around and marched into the house.

Scott watched him go. It was all he could do to keep from running into the house and snatching the letter from his father's hand. The door swung open again and his father reappeared. "You'd better get that lawn mowed before you go to work."

"Of course," Scott said sarcastically.

"Don't use that tone of voice with me."

Without another word, Scott walked to the garage and retrieved the lawn mower. He began pushing it down the driveway toward the front lawn when his father yelled at him, "And do a better job than last week. It's about time you took some pride in your work."

Fuming, Scott mowed the front lawn. The lawn mower clicked like a metronome as the blades twirled. Once the grass catcher was full, he removed it and carried it back to the garbage can next to the garage.

His father came out of the house. "I assume you're going to sweep up that trail of grass you've left behind," he growled from the porch.

Scott looked at where he walked and saw a couple of small clumps of grass that had fallen from the grass catcher. Silently, he kicked them back onto the lawn.

His father shook his head. "That's like sweeping dirt under the rug." He stepped down from the porch and walked angrily up to his son. "Do it right." He grabbed Scott by the shoulder and tried to push him down onto the lawn.

"Leave me alone," Scott spat.

"Then do what you're told to do."

It took all of Scott's reserve not to push back at his father.

"What's going on?" His mother's voice trilled across the yard.

Scott pushed his father's hand off his shoulder. "Nothing, Mom. Dad's just telling me how to cut the grass." His voice was as cold as a glacier.

Mutely, his father spun on his heel and walked toward the porch. He looked back over his shoulder and glared at Scott. "How did we raise such a stupid kid? He can't even cut the grass right."

"Randall, we all make mistakes," Colleen said softly.

Scott stood shaking in anger. "Then do it yourself," he said under his breath.

CHAPTER 15

Saturday, December 19, 2015

The smell of bacon wafted into the bedroom and forced Scott's eyelids open. He flexed his shoulders and tried to work the stiffness from them as he crawled out of bed. He crossed the hallway to the bathroom and stepped into the shower. He let water course over his body—as hot as he could stand—and wash the road weariness from him. He slipped on a pair of khaki pants and a T-shirt before making his way down the hall to the kitchen. Jill faced the sink while bacon sizzled in a frying pan on the stove.

"Good morning," he said.

Without turning, Jill nodded her head slightly.

"I heard your kids got here last night."

"Yes."

Awkwardly, Scott pulled out a chair and seated himself at the kitchen table. Silence filled the room with the exception of the frying bacon and the sound of a wooden spoon clicking against the shallow bowl. Jill finished mixing the pancake batter and set the bowl down next to the stove.

"Anything I can do to help?" Scott asked.

"No," she replied flatly. She bent down, opened the cupboard door beneath the sink, and pulled several sheets of paper towels from a roll. She folded the towels, set them on the counter, and with a fork, lifted the bacon out of the pan and placed the slices on the folded towels. Without a word, she poured the bacon fat into an empty orange juice can, returned the frying pan to the stove, and poured some of the pancake batter into it.

"What time do we need to be at the church?" Scott asked, breaking the silence.

"The viewing starts at 9:45, but you don't have to be there at all," she snapped at him. "I don't think anyone will miss you."

Scott moistened his lips with his tongue. "Jill, listen, I know you have every right to be mad at me, but . . ."

She spun around and pointed the fork at Scott. "Oh, really. Why would you think that? Where were you when Dad's mind began to fail? Where were you when Mom broke her hip? Where have you been while the rest of us have tried to keep a family together? Where, Scott?"

"Look, Jill, I know I haven't been a very good member of the family."

"Very good? You haven't even been a member as far as I can tell. You've just been some vague memory of the past that Mom and Dad wanted to remember." She shook the fork at him.

"I, I don't know what to say."

"Well, you haven't said much in the past. I've never seen even a Christmas card from you. We didn't know whether you were alive or dead. Now you show up and everything is supposed to be forgiven?" She spread both hands. "Where have you been, anyway? Dad tried to find you. He even hired a private detective to find you. But, oh no, you were determined to disappear, and you did a pretty darn good job of it."

Scott slumped in his chair and put his head in his hands. "It hasn't been easy for me, either," he said weakly.

"Oh, poor you," Jill said as she flipped the pancake. Silence descended like a block of ice. After a moment or two Jill reached in the cupboard above the sink and removed a plate. She slipped the pancake onto it and added a couple of strips of bacon. She placed the food in front of Scott. "Well, dear brother, have some breakfast; or is that too much for you to swallow?" She spun around and marched out of the kitchen.

Scott looked for a pot of coffee, then realized where he was. He poured some orange juice from the pitcher on the table and began eating his breakfast. *I made a mistake coming home,* he thought. *But I had to see for myself that he was dead.*

He had nearly finished eating when Jill pushed his mother's chair into the room. "Good morning, Scott," his mother said. "Oh, good, Jill has fed you already."

"She's taken care of me," he said flatly.

She wheeled her chair up to the table. "Jill, just before we went to bed, Scott was about to tell me where he's been. This will keep him from having to repeat the story." She patted the back of his hand. "So, where have you been?"

Jill poured some more batter into the frying pan. "This ought to be good," she said under her breath.

"Well, after I was kicked out," he began.

"Kicked out?" Jill laughed. "You, the favorite son."

Scott felt the anger rising. "Listen, Jill, you can play the injured sister all you want, but it isn't going to work."

She slammed the frying pan down on the stove, whipped off her apron, and marched out of the kitchen. "Mom, you need to be at the church before ten. Call me if 'wonder boy' can't give you a ride." A moment later, the front door slammed.

Scott's mother pursed her lips. "That didn't go too well," she said softly. "Would you mind getting me a pancake and some bacon?"

"No problem. What's with her anyway?"

"I don't know; I think everything has kind of piled up on her."

Scott felt the anger dissipating like smoke. "I'm sure it hasn't been easy." Guilt welled up in his chest. He finished cooking a pancake and slipped it onto a dish with some bacon. He sat down across the table from his mother.

"Thank you." She bowed her head and offered a prayer. Scott felt mildly uncomfortable. He couldn't remember the last time he'd prayed.

When she finished saying grace, she began eating her breakfast. Scott watched her eat in silence. After a few moments he asked softly, "Mom, you seem to accept his passing pretty well. I haven't seen any tears."

She laid her fork down. "Scott, the tears were shed long ago when your father's mind began to fail. This is really a blessing." She paused with a wan smile on her lips. "Oh, I'll miss him, but I can't believe the joy he must be feeling with his mind restored."

"I can't imagine what you've gone through."

She picked up her fork and continued eating her meal. "No, you can't. I don't mean this as anything negative, but you weren't here and I'm sure you can't imagine what his life was like."

"Mom . . ."

"Scott, don't beat yourself up. I'm not sure why you were gone for so long; you must have had your reasons. But I'm not sure I totally understand why we never heard a word from you." A tear made its way down her weathered cheek. "I thought you were dead." She sniffled. "No, that's not true; somehow I knew you were alive."

Silence descended over the two of them. Finally Scott whispered, "Mom, I'm sorry, but I just couldn't put up with it anymore."

Colleen waited for her son to say more, but he just sat slumped in his chair.

CHAPTER 16

Saturday, December 19, 2015

Scott lifted his mother into the front seat of his truck, folded her wheelchair, and put it into the covered bed of the Ford. Six inches of snow had fallen through the night and he cleaned off the windows with a brush he kept behind his seat. Carefully, he backed out of the driveway, "I'll shovel the walks after the funeral," he said.

"That would be helpful," his mother replied. She glanced at her son. "Just like old times."

They pulled into the church parking lot five minutes later. Scott retrieved the wheelchair, snapped it open, and lifted his mother carefully from the cab of the truck. Once she was settled comfortably, he pushed her into the building.

"There seemed to be a lot of people at the viewing last night," Scott said as he wheeled his mother into the Relief Society room. He glanced at his father's form in the open coffin. He examined his face; it seemed so relaxed, so unlike the stern, unsmiling countenance he'd grown used to.

"Yes, it was wonderful to see all of those old friends again." She took her son's hands in hers. "As difficult as it might be for you to understand, he was well loved by a lot of people."

Before Scott could respond, a man entered the room and made a beeline for his mother. "Sister Colleen, how are you holding up?"

"Just fine, Bishop." She turned toward Scott. "This is my son Scott, Bishop. Scott, this is Bishop Crawford. His family moved here about fifteen years ago."

The bishop took Scott's hand in his. "I didn't know you had a son, Colleen."

"He's been out of state for a long time," she replied with a smile. "We're glad to have him home again."

The bishop nodded his head. "Does this mean you'd like to change who's giving the family prayer?"

Scott felt a jolt of terror run through him like an electric shock. He put up his hand to protest.

"No, we'll still have Randall's grandson offer it." His mother nodded her head slightly. "Unless you'd like to offer it, Scott; I'm sure Jim would understand."

"No, no, that's fine. I wouldn't want to upset the apple cart." Suddenly, he remembered the first time he'd offered the sacrament prayer after being ordained a priest. He'd offered the prayer on the bread and had added the phrase, "That was shed for them." It was one of the few times his father had attended church with the family, and after Scott had to repeat the prayer, he knew his father wouldn't let him forget it. On the way home, after church, his father said, "Way to go, embarrassing the whole family. Can't you even read a card right?"

"Randall, every one of the priests has made that mistake. Relax," Colleen said.

Scott never offered either of the sacrament prayers again on the infrequent times his father came to church. He always begged off. There was no way he was going to offer a family prayer at his father's funeral. He wasn't even sure what people said in these circumstances.

"You sent Jim home last night before I arrived. I guess I'll meet his family today," Scott said.

His mother smiled at him, "They ought to be here any minute—the viewing is supposed to start in a quarter of an hour."

As if on cue, a couple stepped through the door of the Relief Society room and made their way to the open casket. Tears streamed down both their cheeks as the woman rested her hands on the side of the casket. "Grandpa," she said through her tears, "We're going to miss you." She bent and kissed the still form on his forehead before turning to Scott's mother. "Grandma," was all she said.

"Jenny, this is your uncle Scott," she said.

The girl's eyes opened wide. "You're alive," she exclaimed.

"Afraid so," Scott said with embarrassment. "You're Jill's daughter?"

Jenny nodded her head and then after catching her breath said, "This is my husband, Gordon. We live in Sacramento."

Scott took the proffered hand and shook it. "Pleased to meet you," he said uncomfortably. "I lived in Sacramento for a while."

"Really? When was that?"

"A long time ago—1983."

"That was before I met your niece. We didn't move there until about ten years ago."

Gordon let go of Scott's hand, then bent and kissed Colleen on the cheek. "Mixed emotions?" he asked.

She nodded her head. "Everyone seems to ask that. I've never felt lonelier in my life, but I can't help but feel joy for Randall." She squeezed her son-in-law's hand, "Thank you for just dropping everything and driving up here."

"No problem. I guess it was something we all knew was inevitable, but it still is a shock. Granddad was such a hale and healthy guy, it was hard to see him going downhill."

Another couple scurried into the room. "Grandma," the young man said as he bent and kissed her cheek. "Are you holding up okay?"

Colleen nodded her head. "Better than expected, I think. Jim, this is your uncle Scott."

Jim stepped backward as if he'd been shocked. "Really?"

"Really," Scott said. "Hard to believe, but really."

Jim recovered enough to shake Scott's hand. "This is my wife, Meg." A strikingly beautiful woman smiled shyly at Scott. She was clearly several months pregnant.

"Meg, it's good to meet you."

"Where's Mom?" Jim asked.

"Running late as usual," Jenny offered. "You know what Grandma says all the time, 'It's good Jill was born two weeks early, because she hasn't been on time to anything since.'"

A few people were entering the Relief Society room, and Scott quickly arranged his mother at the head of the casket. Jill burst through the door and took her place on the other side of her mother as a distinguished-looking gentleman extended his hand. "I'm Ronald Prince," he said.

"I'm Scott."

Colleen reached for the man's hand. "Bishop, how good to see you again." She turned to Scott. "Bishop Prince was called as bishop when Bishop Fullmer was released about twenty-five years ago."

Scott nodded his head as he tried to remember who Bishop Fullmer was. "Oh."

"We're going to miss that old rascal," Bishop Prince said, looking at Richard in the casket. "I wish I'd visited him more often. I feel kind of guilty."

"Oh, Bishop, he wouldn't have recognized you, I'm afraid." She looked up at Scott. "Bishop Prince and his family moved to Cedar City just after he was released." She looked back at Bishop Prince. "How is your family, anyway?"

"The older three are all married. Ben's on a mission in San Jose. We have six grandchildren with one more on the way."

She shook her head. "It seems like just yesterday your little kids were climbing on your lap, and now three are married. I remember teaching Ben in Primary—Sunbeams if I remember right. You've been gone nearly fifteen years." She smiled at the memory. "It's so good of you to come."

Bishop Prince nodded his head, "When I saw the obituary in the paper I was shocked. *The Deseret News* does make it to Cedar City, you know. I always thought Randall would outlive me. He was such a good man."

"Yes, he was," Colleen replied.

Scott felt his jaw tighten.

"Mildred wanted to come, but she has trouble sitting for a long time." Bishop Prince took Jill's hand in his. "How are you doing, beautiful?"

Jill looked into this kind man's face as said, "Struggling with a whole raft of emotions, Bishop."

"I understand."

She glanced at Scott. "I'm not sure you do," she said under her breath.

With a slight shrug, the former bishop let go of her hand and stopped at the head of the casket.

A growing line extended out the door of the Relief Society room. Scott watched it grow in awe. *Why in the world are all these people coming to his viewing? Either they're as glad to see him go as I am, or something really changed.*

CHAPTER 17

Saturday, December 19, 2015

Scott was relieved that with his niece and nephew in place he wasn't the first in the line. The throng of people coming to honor his father snaked out the door into the hallway. Most of the people seemed to be members of the ward. Some of them Scott even remembered.

A small, white-haired gentleman, bent with age, leaned on his cane as he approached Scott. He looked up at Scott's face with rheumy eyes. "Do I know you?" he wheezed.

"I'm Scott."

It was as if an electric shock went through the frail body. "Really! Why, I thought you'd passed away."

Scott shook his head slowly. "No, but I've been gone for quite a while."

"Your father told me he thought you'd died," the old man persisted.

"He probably hoped I had," Scott said.

"Nonsense." He clasped Scott's hand with both of his. "He was so proud of you." He turned his attention to Scott's mother.

"Colleen, you have been an angel. I can't believe what you must be feeling."

"Oh, Brother Anderson, how good of you to come."

He looked past her at the body lying in the coffin. "We had so many good times together." He nodded his head. "And some tough times."

Colleen nodded her head in response. "You were one of his favorites, LeRoy."

"I never could understand why he wanted me as his counselor."

"Because he knew what a wonderful, kind man you are."

Brother Anderson twisted his head and looked at the line behind him. "I'm holding things up. I'm always there if you need anything, understand?"

"Thank you. You're so kind."

People genuinely seemed moved by the passing of Randall Simms.

Bishop Crawford approached his mother. "Sister Simms, I don't want to turn any of these people away, but it's time for the family prayer. Unless you feel differently, I'm going to close the doors and encourage those still in line to make their way to the chapel."

"Of course, Bishop."

Five minutes later, the family was alone in the room with Bishop Crawford. "These are always bittersweet moments. We all feel a loss being parted temporarily from a loved one. Yet, it was no secret that Brother Randall had suffered immensely during these past few years, as have you, Colleen."

Scott noticed all the others were nodding their heads in agreement. *Payback, Dad,* he thought.

After the bishop spoke a few more words, he invited Jim to offer the family prayer, following which the coffin was closed and the procession began from the Relief Society room to the chapel.

Scott fell in line next to his nephew, Gordon. "So you live in Sacramento?"

"Yes. We moved there right after we were married," Gordon said softly. "It was quite an adjustment for Jenny. She really didn't want to be away from her mother, especially after Dan died."

"That must have been hard on everyone," Scott replied.

"It was doubly hard on Jen; we'd only been married two months when her dad died, and we were moving away from everything she knew and everybody she loved."

Scott nodded his head. They were nearly to the chapel when he said, "I can understand how she felt. It's tough to leave everything behind."

Gordon nodded his head. "She really hated to leave her grandpa. He was her idol."

Scott shook his head slowly as they moved to their appointed seats.

"Sacramento's a beautiful town. How come you left?" Gordon said.

Bishop Crawford pulled the microphone down and cleared his throat.

"It's a long story," Scott whispered back. He was happy the service was beginning and he didn't have to explain any further.

CHAPTER 18

Monday, January 2, 1984

Scott pulled the apron over his head and took his place next to the grill. He'd volunteered to do a double shift at McDonald's so that some of the employees with families could spend the holiday at home. With his year's experience at Bear's Burger Bar, he'd fallen into the routine at McDonald's quite easily. By the time the end of the summer came, he'd been promoted to floor manager.

Juan Cabral had turned out to be a delightful roommate. He was easygoing and had a wicked sense of humor. The basement apartment they occupied wasn't opulent by any sense of the word, but it sufficed. There were two bedrooms, a kitchen, and a bathroom with a shower. They'd found a used television set at Goodwill for ten dollars and a small table for another five dollars. Between them they'd found common appetites for breakfast cereal, and generally they ate lunch and dinner at work.

Scott tied the apron strings around his waist and threw the first hamburger patties on the grill. They sizzled and spat grease at him. The timer on the fryer buzzed and he lifted the basket of french fries out of the boiling oil. He was surprised at how busy they were for early afternoon on a holiday. New Year's Day had fallen on Sunday this year, and the holiday was being celebrated today.

Roland Maxwell, the manager, walked up behind Scott and handed him an envelope with his paycheck. "You guys all right if I take off?"

Scott nodded his head. "Sure. Thanks for the check."

Roland clapped him on the shoulder. "I wish it were more, but you get what you get, I guess." With a wink, he headed out the back door.

An hour later, Scott had a short break and he pulled the pay envelope out of his pocket. "Three hundred twenty dollars," he said under his breath. "I'll cash this tomorrow and I'll have over a thousand saved." His part of the rent was fifty dollars a month, and after paying for food, he was able to save a good portion of his check each two weeks.

The lights came on in the restaurant as the sun set. "Craig," Juan said. "Can you take over the cash register?"

"Sure, Juan." He slipped off his apron and took his spot behind the register. He heard the "shush" of the door as it opened and two young men entered. Both were wearing suits, and on their breast pockets were the unmistakable black and white name tags of missionaries. Scott recognized one of them, Robert Johanssen, who lived half a mile away from his folks' home in Bountiful.

They scanned the lighted menus above the grill before stepping up to the register. "What can I get you gentlemen?" Scott asked.

"I'll take a number five . . ." Robert paused and looked quizzically at Scott. "Hey, aren't you Scotty Simms?"

Scott's heart raced and he struggled to keep a neutral face. "Sorry, my name's Craig." He tapped his name tag with his index finger.

"Man, you look just like this kid I went to school with. We had AP biology together."

"Must be my doppelgänger," Scott said as nonchalantly as he could with a shrug of his shoulders.

"You even sound just like him. I was a year ahead of him, but . . ." The elder shook his head. "You could pass for him."

Scott smiled. "I hope he was a nice guy. You wanted a number five. What drink do you want with that?"

He finished taking their orders and tried to remain calm. By the end of his shift he knew that it was time to move on. He was sure Elder Johanssen would mention seeing him to his parents, and that information might get passed on to his father. The next day, he told Roland Maxwell that he had a family emergency and had to quit. He made the same excuse to Juan Cabral.

The next bus out of town took him to Phoenix.

CHAPTER 19

Saturday, December 19, 2015

Except for those seats reserved for the family, every seat in the chapel was full. Not only was the overflow filled, but the doors into the cultural hall had been opened to accommodate the crowd. He and his nephew sat next to his mother. Jill and the rest of her family sat down on the other side. The flag-draped coffin lay in front of the pulpit.

Bishop Crawford invited the congregation to be seated. "Brothers and sisters, welcome. My name is James Crawford, the bishop of the ward. Behind me on the stand are my counselors and the members of the stake presidency. President Walter Conway is presiding at this meeting." He looked back over his shoulder and nodded at the men who were seated on the stand. "Today we are gathered here to celebrate the life of Randall Simms. In the event you did not get a printed program, let me quickly go over the services.

"The family prayer was offered by a grandson, Jim Palmer. The opening hymn will be number 293, "Each Life That Touches Ours for Good," with Sister Carol Bangerter at the organ and Sister Patty Salmon directing the singing. The opening prayer will be given by Meghan Simms, a granddaughter. We will then hear from Gordon Burrell, a grandson, who will give a brief eulogy. Following Brother Burrell, we will have a musical number, "O My Father," performed on the flute

by Sister Luella Parsons, accompanied by Sister Carol Bangerter."
The bishop sat down and the organ began to play.

Scott found it hard to explain the feelings he was experiencing.
Thirty-two years had passed since he'd entered a chapel and yet everything seemed so familiar. Unbidden tears sprang from his eyes as he
listened to the words of the opening song:

> *Each life that touches ours for good*
> *Reflects thine own great mercy, Lord;*
> *Thou sendest blessings from above*
> *Thru words and deeds of those who love.*

The tune was familiar even after all these years. Scott could even
remember a few of the words, but he found himself incapable of
joining in the singing—it was if his throat had closed until his voice
was a mere squeak. When the hymn finished, his niece slipped out of
the pew and made her way to the pulpit.

Her prayer was simple and sweet. She thanked God for the
opportunity to have known her grandfather and for the loving, kind
man he had been. She asked for comfort for the family and expressed
thanks for all the friends who had helped her grandmother through
these troubling times.

Scott closed his eyes and bowed his head. This was not the father
he remembered. His father was neither loving nor kind. When
Meghan finished the prayer, Gordon stood and shuffled out of the
pew. He waited until Meghan had seated herself before he climbed
the steps to the pulpit. He reached into his suit pocket and removed
a folded piece of paper.

"Randall Simms was born November 10, 1935, in Woods Cross,
Utah, the son of Raymond Simms and Nora Ellen Page Simms. He
was the eldest of three boys. He spent his younger years in Woods
Cross until the family moved to Bountiful when he was eight years of
age. He graduated from Davis High School and then enlisted in the
military. He was sent to Korea just before the end of the war. When

he returned, he enrolled in the University of Utah and graduated with an engineering degree. He was a mechanical engineer with Simco Fabricating until he retired.

"He married Colleen Simonsen on March 18, 1960. Their marriage was later solemnized in the Salt Lake Temple. Randall and Colleen were the parents of two children, Scott and Jill, and are the grandparents of two grandchildren.

"He was preceded in death by his parents and both brothers, Ronald and Roy. A faithful member of The Church of Jesus Christ of Latter-day Saints, he served in many callings including bishop and high councilor. He will be missed by the many people whose lives he touched."

Scott's head snapped up. *Bishop? My father had been a bishop?* He sat in shocked silence.

Gordon folded the obituary and slipped it back into his coat pocket. "There is supposed to be an old Chinese curse, 'May you live in interesting times.' These last five years of Grandpa's life have been interesting to say the least. Those of you who have visited him in the past little while have found that he might or might not have recognized you. Frequently, when Jenny and I visited, he would call me Roy. I finally realized Roy was his brother who was killed in Vietnam. Grandpa would tell me that the rest home he was in was a pretty good hotel he lived in. You could take a bath anytime you wanted to. And he thought the food was pretty good too."

Gentle laughter filled the chapel. Gordon grasped the pulpit with both hands. "But that isn't the Randall Simms that I first knew.

"As I got to know Grandpa while I was dating Jenny, I found this bright, inquisitive person who would go out of his way to help others. He was the most compassionate person I've ever met. When Dan, my father-in-law, died, it was Grandpa who comforted his grieving daughter and supported her through the clouds of gloom and depression. It was Grandpa who always made us feel as if we were the most important people in the world—every one of us. And

I can tell we are not alone. I am so impressed by how many people stopped at the viewing to tell me how Randall had affected their lives.

"This is the Randall Simms I remember and will always remember." He said a few more words, closed his eulogy, and returned to his seat.

Immediately, a tall, dark-haired woman rose, walked to the piano, and picked up her flute. Sister Bangerter took her place at the keyboard, and the haunting notes of "O My Father" filled the room.

My father a bishop? Scott shook his head. *That's hard to believe— the way he felt about bishops.*

CHAPTER 20

Sunday, June 3, 1979

Scott raced through the front door into the living room. "Mom, guess what?" He loosened his necktie.

His mother was in the kitchen finishing their Sunday meal. "What, honey?"

Scott smiled broadly as he sashayed into the kitchen. "Bishop Gerber wants me to be secretary in the teachers quorum."

"Oh, Scotty, that's wonderful. Imagine that, when you've only been in the quorum for less than two months."

At that moment, Randall wandered into the kitchen. He still had a couple of sections of the newspaper in his hand. "What's wonderful?" he asked.

"Scotty's been called as the secretary to the teachers quorum."

"How come?" Randall grumbled.

Scott shrugged his shoulders. "Don't know. Bishop Gerber asked me."

"Well, tell him no. I don't trust him."

Scott's shoulders slumped. "How come?"

"You know what he does for a living. He runs that appliance shop and I hear he takes advantage of people."

Colleen spoke up, "In what way?"

Randall turned around and walked out of the room. "Any way he can," he said over his shoulder.

Scott looked as if he was about to cry. "Honey, just wait a little bit, I think your father might change his mind." Colleen patted him on his shoulder. "Now, why don't you go slip into something more comfortable? Dinner will be ready in a couple of minutes."

Scott made his way to his room and threw himself on the bed. *Why does he always have to find something wrong with everything I do?*

He was still lying on the bed when his mother called out, "Scotty, Jill, time for dinner."

Randall sat at the head of the table with a roast in front of him. He sliced a piece for each of them and sent the plates around the table. Colleen added a scoop of mashed potatoes and poured gravy over both the meat and potatoes. Then she added a spoonful of green beans.

Silently, they ate their meal. When they finished, Jill and Scott cleared the table while Colleen brought in a chocolate cake, which she sliced and served. While they were eating dessert, Randall broke the silence.

"You know Bishop Gerber isn't the worst cheater. Colleen, do you remember Bishop Anderson? He was a piece of work."

"He seemed like a good man to me," she replied.

Randall snorted. "Helped that shyster that took all that money from those old ladies in the rest home. Don't you remember?"

Colleen shook her head. "No, I don't. Where did you hear that?"

"Everybody knew about it. I can't believe you didn't." With that, he stood up and strode out of the room.

Scott stared after his father and then his mother said, "Don't give up, yet." She smiled at her son.

Nothing more was said during the week, but on Sunday morning, as Scott prepared to go to church, his father said, "I guess you can be secretary if you want to. Just be careful what the bishop asks you to do. Once those guys get into office they're just like politicians; they let the power go to their heads."

CHAPTER 21

Saturday, December 19, 2015

Scott watched as Bishop Crawford stepped up to the microphone. "That was beautiful, Sister Parsons. We'll now hear from Brother Anthony Mitchell and Sister Caroline Frazier. Following Sister Frazier's remarks, we'll sing the closing hymn, "God Be With You Till We Meet Again," hymn number 152. The closing prayer will be offered by Patriarch Lloyd Allred." He nodded toward a man sitting on the stand. "Brother Mitchell."

Anthony Mitchell was barely tall enough to see over the pulpit. Bishop Crawford lowered it until it rested on its base. Brother Mitchell reached up and pulled the microphone down toward his mouth. "Brothers and sisters, this is such an honor to be asked to speak at my dear friend's funeral. Colleen, I don't know what I can do to repay you for extending this opportunity to me."

He adjusted his rimless spectacles. "All of you knew Randall Simms and all of the lives he touched. I suspect that in some way he touched each of you. My first recollection of him was when we served together on the scout committee. We both thought it peculiar since neither one of us had a boy in the scouting program. But we rolled up our sleeves and went to work.

"Neither one of us knew much about the program, but it didn't take long until Randall had researched everything he could about scouting and realized the value that being an Eagle Scout could mean in a young man's life. He set a goal right then and there that every young man in our ward would achieve his Eagle. Nearly six years later when we were released and called to other positions, we had watched thirteen young men achieve that rank.

"However, the most amazing thing that happened during that time did not have to do with scouting at all. You older members of the ward would remember my wife, Rozella." Brother Mitchell paused for a moment to collect himself. "She was diagnosed with cancer—stage 4 pancreatic cancer. The doctors gave her six months to a year to live. I was beside myself—scared to death about what lay ahead. Randall put his arm around me and became my savior. I'm sure few of you knew that he came to our house and single-handedly remodeled our bedroom so that it could accommodate Rozella's hospital bed. Two or three nights each week he stopped on his way home from work to check on her. He and Colleen brought food, took care of our dog when we had to take Rozella for treatments, and kept our lawn mowed—all of those things you don't have time to think about in the middle of all that stress."

Brother Mitchell paused again and then continued, "When Randall was called as bishop, I sustained him enthusiastically. When he asked me to be his counselor, I was surprised and humbled. For five years I watched him as he took care of this ward and all of its members."

He pulled a tissue from the box next to the pulpit, removed his glasses, and dabbed his eyes. "The hardest thing, besides the loss of my sweetheart, that I've ever had to watch was seeing Randall suffer these last five years from Alzheimer's. He was such a student of the scriptures—he could quote them at will—and suddenly it was as if he disappeared."

Brother Mitchell looked into Colleen's eyes. "How we'll miss him, but how happy, how overjoyed we will be when we are reunited with him and see him with all of his faculties restored."

Scott listened intently. What had happened to his father?

Brother Mitchell finished his talk, and Sister Frazier took her place at the microphone. She was much younger than Brother Mitchell and much taller.

"Colleen, I've pondered what I could say ever since you asked me to speak." She looked over the vast congregation. "I have been Colleen's visiting teacher for the past six or seven years," she said in explanation. "I have watched this family draw together to deal with this devastating illness that consumed Brother Simms. When we first moved into the ward, I was so impressed with the Simms family. Not only was Brother Simms there helping us move in, but Sister Simms also brought dinner and fed our family. We have been blessed immeasurably to have known them. When Brother Simms's memory began to fade, I watched with fascination as Sister Simms picked up the responsibilities with grace and poise. If there is a message I've gained from the Simms family, it is simply this, *Service is love in action.*"

Scott shook his head slowly again. *My father giving service? The only time he did anything for anybody else was when he'd get some reward.*

CHAPTER 22

Monday, May 26, 1975

Scott struggled to hold up his end of the girder he and Richard were hauling into the playground. He was big for a ten-year-old, but the piece of equipment was heavy.

"Don't drop it," his father commanded. "Bring it right over here."

Scott and Richard laid the girder at Randall's feet. "Is that where you want it?" Scott asked.

"I suppose it will do," Randall said. He and Richard's father, Robert, lifted the yellow-painted metal girder into place. A second one was positioned parallel to it and rings were hung between the two on sturdy chains.

"It's starting to come together, Randall," Robert said as he wiped the sweat from his head and replaced his hat.

"Yes, it is. I'm glad the weather has held up for us. Sometimes Memorial Day can be pretty wet. I kind of thought it would be raining."

Robert started walking across the schoolyard to where the playground equipment had been unloaded. Randall called after him, "Let the boys bring it. It will be good for them to be part of this."

"It's pretty heavy, Randall."

A cloud seemed to come over Randall's face. "I'm sure they can handle it."

Robert shrugged his shoulders. "I just thought we'd speed things up if we helped." He looked around the parking lot. "I wonder where the rest of the committee members are?"

Randall smirked. "I knew we couldn't count on them. I'm glad we took charge."

"You took charge," Robert said.

Scott and Richard finished hauling a section of pipe and dropped it at Randall's feet. "Not here, Scott, over where those concrete blocks have been set." He pointed at the large sandbox where swings were going to be erected. Dutifully, the boys picked up the pipe and carried it to where Scott's father had pointed.

Piece by piece, the boys carried the equipment from the parking lot to the playground while their fathers put it together. The day wore on, but by late afternoon, the swings, monkey bars, rings, and slides were all in place.

"Just in time," Randall said. A van with a Channel 5 logo on its side pulled into the parking lot and three people climbed out. One of them removed a box from the back of the van, opened it, and removed a television camera. One of the others carried a box full of equipment across the lawn. The third adjusted her hair and freshened her makeup. When she was finished, she walked briskly across the lawn.

"Mr. Simms?" the reporter asked. "I'm Julie Anderson."

Robert Newman pointed at Randall. "He's the guy you're looking for."

Randall smiled broadly and extended his hand. "Nice to meet you."

"Well, this is quite the project. Let me get the camera set up and I'll be ready to interview you."

The cameraman looked at the late afternoon sun, suggested they move closer to the playground slide, and set up a tripod for his camera. The other technician ran a cable from the camera to a microphone with the Channel 5 logo on it. "Sound check," he said as he handed the microphone to the reporter.

"One, two, three," she said. The cameraman checked the meters on his camera and nodded his head.

"Okay, Mr. Simms, if you'll step right over here. Now, don't look at the camera, look at me. We're going to have a conversation, and I'll start by introducing you. I will look at the camera to do that; and then I'll just ask you a few questions about how you were able to build this wonderful playground for the children at this school."

Randall smiled broadly and moved to the spot Julie had indicated.

"Sound check," the technician said.

Julie put the microphone in front of Randall's face. "Count to ten," she said.

"One, two, three, four . . ."

"That will do," the technician said. "We're ready when you're ready."

Julie looked directly into the camera.

"On one," the cameraman said, "Three, two, one."

"This is Julie Anderson at Washington Elementary School, where Randall Simms, a father of one of the students, has been able to raise the funds to build a playground for the school." She turned toward Randall. "Mr. Simms, this is spectacular."

Randall smiled. "We're proud of it."

"Tell us about the project. How did it get started?"

"Well, I could see a need and thought with a little planning we could make it happen. So we asked for donations, bought the equipment, and after some tough negotiations, today we put it together."

"I understand you have a son going to school here."

"A son and a daughter. Both of them will enjoy the use of the playground."

"As well as all of the other students, I'm sure."

"Of course."

"And you've had to do it all yourselves. I'm surprised the school district didn't have people here to help erect the equipment."

Randall shook his head slightly. "On a holiday? Really? We were able to do the whole thing."

"One last thing, Mr. Simms. I understand there is some thought of naming this playground after you."

Randall feigned surprise. "That's not necessary, but if it happens, I'd be honored."

"Thank you. This is Julie Anderson reporting from Washington Elementary School in Bountiful. Back to the studio."

"I think that went well," Julie said. "We'll get it edited and it should be on the news tonight. We're cutting it pretty close for the six o'clock, but I'm sure it will be on by ten."

Randall beamed. "Thanks for coming." Almost as an after-thought, he struck his forehead with the palm of his hand. "Ms. Anderson, I should have introduced you to Robert Newman. He's the other father who helped erect the playground."

"Oh, I'm sorry. I wish I'd known sooner, we'd have interviewed you as well."

"No problem," Robert said with a shake of his head. "Where did you hear about them naming the park after Randall?"

Julie's brow wrinkled. "I'm not sure. I think it was some anony-mous information that was sent to the station along with the request to cover the event." The cameraman whistled loudly and beckoned her to the van. "I'm sorry, I've got to go. Thank you for your time. This really is impressive." She hurried across the lawn to the waiting van.

Scott watched the van pull away. "I wonder who told them about this?" he said gesturing with his hand.

"I have no idea," his father said.

"Come on, Richard, let's head home," Robert said with a shake of his head. Very softly he said, "I might have some idea."

"I think I'm going to let you stay up to watch the news tonight," Randall said as he and Scott walked the two blocks home.

CHAPTER 23

Saturday, December 19, 2015

Sister Frazier concluded her remarks, and Bishop Crawford approached the pulpit. "Before we sing the closing song, with your indulgence I'd like to conclude by offering a few remarks. I have known the Simms family since my family moved here twenty-one years ago. The first people to welcome us into the ward were Brother and Sister Simms. The moving van had barely backed into our driveway before they showed up to help us move in. In fact, because we hadn't finished unloading the van by dinnertime, we were invited to dinner at the Simmses' home. My wife and I were talking about this last evening after the viewing, and she reminded me we actually slept in their home the first night because our beds weren't set up yet.

"When Brother Simms was called as bishop, I wasn't the least bit surprised. There was no one more deserving in the ward. And over the next five years, I watched him shepherd this ward through some pretty tough times. Regardless of the situation, Bishop Simms was always there offering a helping hand."

Bishop Crawford cleared his throat as he struggled with his emotions. "When our son, Ed, was severely wounded in the Gulf War, Bishop Simms spent countless hours comforting us; and when our son returned home, Bishop Simms helped arrange for transportation to the rehab center. When no one else was available, he showed up to take Ed himself. I'm sure we aren't the only ones for whom his selfless service was spent."

Scott bowed his head and tried to comprehend that this was the same person who had driven him out of the house. He felt his mother's gaze, turned his head toward her, and saw her smiling. She gave a gentle nod of her head.

Bishop Crawford continued on with his remarks about Randall until he concluded with his testimony of the reality of the resurrection and his knowledge that they would all be able to see Randall Simms again.

Then he closed the service by saying, "We will now sing the closing hymn, number 152, "God Be with You Till We Meet Again,"followed by the closing prayer."

The congregation sang the familiar hymn, and the stake patriarch offered the closing prayer. Bishop Crawford invited the congregation to stand as the coffin was wheeled out of the chapel. Members of the high council had been asked to serve as pallbearers, and they fell in line behind the members of the family. Scott pushed his mother's wheelchair to the waiting limousine. Gently, he lifted her into the back seat, folded the wheelchair, and placed it in the trunk before he climbed in himself. Jill was already seated next to his mother. A second car contained the rest of the family.

"You looked very surprised," his mother said.

Scott squirmed a little in his seat. "I . . . I just never saw my father the same way all those people did."

Colleen nodded her head. "I told you he'd changed."

Jill glared at Scott. "Like you'd even want to know."

Scott hung his head. "Jill, I don't know how to explain."

"I don't know if I even want to hear it."

Colleen placed her hand on her daughter's arm. "Sweetheart, this isn't the time or place to argue. See if you can put aside your bitterness until you know the whole story."

Jill clamped her mouth shut, folded her arms, and sank back into the seat while they covered the few miles to the cemetery.

Scott took a deep breath and tried to relax. "When was he called as bishop?"

Colleen wiped a tear from her eye. "Your friend, President Newman, called him in 1999. He served for five years. He was a good bishop. The people of the ward loved him."

"That's so hard for me to comprehend. He was always so negative . . . so abrupt."

"When we get home," Colleen said gently, "I'll tell you about the man your father became and how it happened."

The limo turned into the cemetery and drove slowly to the burial site. Half a foot of snow surrounded it. Green carpet had been arranged around the grave, and a dozen folding chairs were set up under a canopy for the family. Many of the people who'd attended the funeral assembled themselves around the grave.

Scott unfolded the wheelchair, placed his mother in it, and pushed it through the snow. When everyone was in place, Bishop Crawford picked up the microphone from a portable speaking system and welcomed the crowd. It was cold, and huge feathery flakes of snow began to fall as Gordon dedicated the grave.

Colleen asked Scott to push her next to the coffin and with her head bowed, she placed her hands on top of the polished wood surface and sobbed.

CHAPTER 24

Saturday, December 19, 2015

Scott wheeled his mother into the front room of her home and lifted her from the wheelchair into her recliner.

"Scott, would you mind turning on the tree lights?" she asked. Scott found the switch and turned them on. "Turn on the stereo and play some Christmas music."

"Any particular CD?"

Colleen shook her head. "No, maybe just turn on the radio to that station that plays Christmas music all day."

A few minutes later the house was filled with the sounds of Christmas. "Anything else, Mom?"

She shook her head, "No. I'm quite comfortable. That lunch the Relief Society provided was delicious." She looked past the Christmas tree to the gently falling snow outside the front window. "A white Christmas. Oh, how your father loved a white Christmas."

Scott seated himself on the couch, leaned forward, and put his hands between his knees. "Today was harder on you than I thought it was going to be."

Colleen nodded her head. "At the cemetery, I finally realized he was really gone."

Scott nodded his head, unsure what, if anything, to say. They sat quietly listening to the music coming from the stereo. The star on the top of the tree blinked on and off.

"Scott, what happened?" Her voice was as thin as a reed in the wind.

Scott shifted uncomfortably on the couch. "We had a disagreement—a major one."

"What kind of disagreement?"

Scott examined the backs of his hands before answering. "When I graduated from high school, I wanted to get a full-time job and start earning my own money. I mean, working at Bear's was okay, but not what I wanted to do with my life."

"I see."

"He wanted me to go to college and become a doctor."

"Well, you certainly had the brains to do that, and you had your scholarship," she replied softly.

"But it wasn't what I wanted to do. I really wanted to be an engineer. Anyway, we had a blow up about it and he told me in no uncertain terms that I was going to be a doctor, and I'd have to do what he said." Scott stood up and walked toward the Christmas tree.

"Do you understand why he said that?" his mother asked softly.

"Because he was always trying to control my life," Scott spat out.

His mother straightened herself in her recliner. "Because he wanted you to be better than he was." She wiped her lips with the tissue in her hand. "You know his father threatened to kick him out of the house when he was a teenager if he didn't follow the rules."

"Like father, like son, I guess."

"Scott, what I'm trying to say is that he didn't have a role model for a father and sometimes he . . ."

"He threatened to throw me out if I didn't do what he said!"

Tears ran down his mother's cheeks. "Scott, he just wanted the best for you. He had his own way of showing love."

Scott snorted. "Love? I can't ever remember him saying he loved me. All he ever did was criticize." He was amazed at the anger that burned in his chest.

There was an uncomfortable silence that followed his outburst. Then his mother said, "Scott, I think we're both tired. It has been an emotional day. I need to tell you about how your father changed, and the sooner the better. Why don't we get some sleep and perhaps we can continue our conversation in the morning."

"I'm sorry, Mom. I don't know why I feel the way I do. I couldn't believe what was being said about him by the speakers today. That wasn't the man I knew."

Colleen spread her hands in front of her. "You're right, honey, that man you knew changed dramatically." She reached for her wheelchair. "Would you help me?"

Scott moved quickly to his mother's side. "Will you help me? I need to know what happened. You said he changed. How did you make him change?"

Colleen settled into her wheelchair. "Oh, Scotty, I didn't change him. The only person you can change is yourself."

As he wheeled her down the hallway toward her bedroom, his mind flashed back to his time in Phoenix and how his life changed.

PART TWO

Phoenix

CHAPTER 25

Thursday, January 5, 1984

ow old are you, Craig?"

"Nineteen," Scott replied.

"What experience have you had?" Steven Bird sat behind his desk with his hands laced behind his head and his legs crossed.

"I've mostly been a fry cook—McDonald's most recently. But I'm a quick study."

"You willing to work nights?"

Scott nodded his head. "That would be perfect." He looked out the window of the shift supervisor's office at the vast warehouse.

"Ever run a forklift?"

Scott shook his head. "No, I haven't. But I'm sure willing to learn."

"You look pretty husky. Our guys have to be able to move fifty-pound boxes all the time. You up to that?"

"Sure."

"How about this. I'll give you the job for the next month. If you work out, you can go permanent. If not . . ." he shrugged his shoulders. "Well, you were looking for a job when you took this one. Okay?"

"Sounds good. When do I start?"

Steven looked at the clock above the door to his office. "This shift ends at eight o'clock. Come back then and I'll introduce you to the foreman. You can start tonight."

The two of them stood up, and Scott shook hands with Steven. "I won't let you down."

"Good."

Scott walked out of the warehouse and took a deep breath. When he'd arrived at the Phoenix bus depot, he'd spotted a rack of free newspapers filled with want ads. On the top of the second page was an opening for a stock boy at the CFI warehouse. He stashed his suitcase in a locker at the station and asked the ticket master how to get to CFI. After a short bus ride, he walked the final two blocks to the warehouse. Now all he had to do was find a place to stay.

Scott looked at his watch—it was nearly five o'clock. "I'll just get something to eat and hang out until eight. After I get off shift, I'll find someplace to stay," he muttered to himself. He was in a warehouse district and he couldn't immediately spot any place to eat. Scott arbitrarily started walking east on the sidewalk. He'd gone for several blocks before he spotted a little mom and pop café. The air smelled of fried onions as he opened the door. A rotund, short, balding man stepped to the counter.

"What can I get for you?" His Spanish accent was pronounced.

Scott looked for a menu and found a blackboard on the wall with today's offerings. "How about your special."

"Hokay," the man said. Scott looked around the dingy room. There was only one other customer, and he was sitting at the counter on a stool. There were four empty booths that lined the wall.

Scott settled into the booth nearest the door and studied the other diner. He appeared to be quite old and was dressed in a ragged overcoat. His hair hung down over his collar. It was the color of cold steel. The man hunched over his cup of coffee and muttered to himself.

A couple of minutes later, the cook brought Scott a plate of beef stew and a slice of bread. "Whatch'a want to drink?"

"What do you have?"

"Coffee, tea, coke, sprite, orange . . ." he said ticking each off on his fingers.

"Sprite would be fine."

The stew turned out to be tasty, and the slab of bread was filling. Scott finished his meal and stepped up to the counter. "How much do I owe you?"

"Two fifty," the man said.

Scott pulled out his wallet and handed the man a five-dollar bill.

"Just a minute." He disappeared back into the kitchen and was gone for several minutes before he returned and handed Scott his change. Scott thought back to all the shifts he'd worked at Bear's and McDonald's and how grateful he'd been for a tip. He handed a dollar bill back to the cook.

"*Gracias*," the man said with a big smile.

"You're welcome. The stew was delicious." Out of the corner of his eye, he saw the other customer watching him closely. He had an uneasy feeling. "Well, I'll be on my way." As he walked toward the door, the other man slipped off his stool and stared at Scott.

Once he was on the sidewalk Scott started moving quickly down the street toward the warehouse. The steel-haired man followed him and kept pace. Darkness fell and the streets were poorly lit. Scott increased his speed and his pursuer did the same. Sweat ran down Scott's back. He tried to remember how many blocks he'd walked from the warehouse, but he wasn't certain. He stared ahead into the darkness and increased his speed again until he was nearly jogging. At the end of the block he could see the CFI warehouse, dimly lit. He could hear footsteps behind him. Suddenly, a hand shot out and grabbed his shoulder from behind.

"Hey, buddy, just hand me your wallet and no one gets hurt."

Scott spun around and faced his assailant. He shielded a knife with his overcoat, but the threat was real. "Okay," Scott said with a shaky voice. "Take it easy." He pulled his wallet from his rear pocket and removed the twenty-two dollars it held. "Here, it's all I have."

The man grabbed the bills from his hand. "Show me," he demanded. Scott opened the wallet and showed him it was empty. He was thankful he'd left nearly a thousand dollars in his suitcase securely locked at the bus station.

Without another word, the man spat on the pavement in front of Scott, turned, and ran. Scott's heart was beating as fast as a snare drum. His knees felt like rubber. Unsteadily, he made his way to the warehouse, pulled open the door, and sank down on the floor.

"You're early," Steven said. "What's the matter?"

"A guy just robbed me," Scott exclaimed.

"I'll call the cops," Steven responded as he grabbed the phone.

"No, that's okay, it was only twenty bucks. He's already gone.

Steven looked down the street through the glass door. "It can be a little rough down here, Craig. You might want to consider driving instead of walking. At least the parking lot's lighted."

CHAPTER 26

Friday, August 31, 1984

Sweat soaked his shirt as he finished stacking the last of the boxes near the rear of the warehouse. He lifted his cap, brushed his hair back from his forehead, and replaced it. He glanced at the time clock—7:30—only half an hour left on his shift. Even this early in the morning the temperature inside the building was well over a hundred degrees. Ceiling fans barely gave any motion to the stagnant air.

Scott parked the forklift and walked to the drinking fountain where his co-worker, Charlie, stood. Charlie swabbed the back of his neck with a bright red kerchief he had stuffed in his back pocket. "Hotter than a preacher's wrath in here. I'm glad we have a holiday Monday."

As the only two workers on the night shift, Charlie and Scott had become friends. Charlie had taught Scott how to operate the forklift and scissor lift they used to store, arrange, and retrieve the freight that rolled in daily.

"Do you have anything planned for Labor Day?" Charlie said as he strolled toward the controls that lowered the tambour door.

Scott shook his head. "Just another day for me."

"Want to come over to my folks' place? They're having a barbecue."

Scott thought for a moment. "I don't want to be a party crasher."

"No problem. I told them I might bring a friend."

"If you're sure."

The door finished closing with a satisfying clank. and Charlie headed back to the forklift. "Want me to pick you up?"

"That would be great."

"Okay, I'll wheel by about noon."

The next day, Scott bundled up his meager batch of clothes and walked the two blocks to the Laundromat down the street from his apartment. He'd found a small back room to rent in a run-down house just outside the warehouse district. The elderly couple, Elden and Harriet Archibald, who owned the house, were happy to take twenty-five dollars a week from him. In return, they often invited him to have dinner with them. Although he was only obligated to work four twelve-hour shifts, he often worked the fifth one for extra pay.

Three months after being robbed, he was still a little nervous about walking the half dozen blocks to work, but his assailant had never reappeared. Several times he had returned to the little café where he had first seen the man, but apparently he was long gone. The owner couldn't even remember him.

The drier finished spinning and Scott removed the clothing, folded it, and carried it carefully back down the street to his apartment. The day was already turning into a scorcher. He was thankful for the air conditioner that clunked and wheezed cool air into the room. His landlord, Elden, knocked on the door that separated Scott's room from the rest of the house.

"Come in."

Elden pushed the door open slowly. "Craig, I just wondered if you had anything planned for the holiday?"

Scott nodded his head. "I've been invited to a party by one of the guys at work. Why?"

"Nothin', just wonderin'."

"Did you need something?"

"No, no, that okay."

When he had a day off, Scott had been pulling the weeds and trying to dress up the old house. One weekend he'd used a steel brush to scrape the flaking paint from the house and then applied a fresh coat of enamel. Elden and Harriet had been in tears. Since that time Scott had run a number of errands for the elderly couple.

"Come on, Elden, what do you need?"

The old man ran his hand through the sparse white hair on his head before answering. "Well, me and Harriet kind of wanted to go over to the Liberty Market in Gilbert."

"Oh. When do you want to go?"

"They're having a Labor Day special on Monday. I'm getting too old to drive that far and, well, we wondered if you could take us?"

Elden owned a vintage 1968 Plymouth Road Runner that had fewer than 30,000 miles on it. He and Harriet had bought it new and kept it in tip-top condition. "When do you want to go?"

"When's your party?"

"Charlie's picking me up at noon."

"Maybe we could go early, if you're willing to drive us."

"I'd be happy to. How early do you want to go?"

"Maybe nine?"

"That would be perfect." With a smile, Elden eased out of the room. Scott put his laundry away before collapsing on the bed. He wondered if he'd ever get used to working the night shift; he seemed perpetually worn out. In no time he was asleep.

CHAPTER 27

Monday, September 3, 1984

Harriet leaned on her walker as she shuffled slowly toward the waiting car. Elden walked behind her while Scott backed the Plymouth out of the slightly sagging garage. He opened the passenger side door and tilted the seat forward. Carefully, Elden folded himself into the back seat. Scott pushed the front seat back into position and helped Harriet into the passenger's seat. She was a diminutive small-boned woman with thinning white hair she pulled back into a bun. Once she was seated, Scott folded her walker and placed it in the trunk before he took his place in the driver's seat.

"You'll need to guide me to where you want to go," he said over his shoulder. "I'm still fairly new to the area."

Elden leaned forward from the back seat and said, "Do you know how to get to the Superstition Freeway?"

Scott nodded his head.

"Stay on it until you get to Gilbert Road, then go south."

A few minutes later, they took the on-ramp to the freeway. Harriett looked out the window at the red soil and desert landscape. "I wonder if they'll ever finish this road. It seems like they've been working on it for such a long time." She turned her head toward Scott. "You're such a dear boy, Craig. We appreciate you driving us."

"No problem," Scott said. "I appreciate you letting me stay with you."

Harriett smiled broadly. "Oh, Craig, you're like the son we never had." Scott smiled in return. "You've never told us where you came from, Craig."

Scott licked his lips before answering. "Sacramento."

"Oh, we have friends who moved to Sacramento," Elden said from the back seat. "I don't suppose you knew the Nielsens?"

Scott shook his head. "It's a pretty big city."

They lapsed into silence for the next few minutes until the Gilbert Road exit appeared. Scott exited the freeway and drove south following Elden's directions. Eventually, they reached Page Avenue and the Liberty Market. Scott pulled into the small parking lot.

"Thank you, thank you, Craig," Harriett said as he retrieved her walker from the trunk and helped her from the car. Elden slowly extricated himself from the back seat and the two of them moved slowly into the market. Scott followed a respectful distance behind. When they entered the store, the man behind the counter waved at them. "That's Sam," said Harriett over her shoulder. "He and his wife, Mary, own the store. They're old friends. Sam and Elden served together in Vietnam." She waved at Sam. "They were two of the older men to go in at the beginning of the war."

As time passed, it became obvious to Scott that along with the shopping, this was more of a social visit between two old friends. There was a lighted clock on the wall behind the counter, and he watched the minutes tick by. The small grocery was filled with customers, and Sam seemed to be able to greet each of them by name. An hour passed. It had taken them about half an hour to drive from their home. It was now quarter to eleven and the time for Charlie to pick him up was drawing near. It didn't seem as if Sam and Elden were going to finish their reminiscing anytime soon.

Harriet saw Scott glancing at the clock. "How soon do we need to leave, Craig, so you can get to your party?"

"By eleven thirty," he said. "But I don't want to interrupt . . ." he trailed off.

"Nonsense, I'll get Elden on the move." She slid her walker across the floor to where the two men were laughing. "Sweetheart, Craig needs to get home soon."

Elden looked up at the clock. "Ten more minutes," he said with a wink.

Harriet slid her walker back to where Scott was standing. "I'll go get him in a few minutes."

Half an hour later she moved to Elden's side. "We need to go. Don't be long, Craig and I will meet you at the car." She moved slowly toward the door and beckoned Scott to follow her. The temperature had increased significantly while they were shopping and the inside of the car felt like an oven. Scott rolled down the windows and helped Harriet into her seat. He could feel sweat soaking into the seat of his pants.

Harriet withdrew a cardboard fan from her purse. She began vigorously fanning her face. After a few minutes, she looked over at Scott. "Craig, you might have to go get Elden before we both melt."

Scott went back into the store and as soon as Elden saw him, he shook hands with Sam and hurried toward the door carrying the small bag of groceries he'd purchased. A few minutes later, he had squeezed into the back seat on the driver's side. "Sorry. I hope I didn't make you late."

Scott started the car. "No problem." He wheeled back onto the road and headed for home. "You two seemed to have a lot to talk about."

"Just catching up." They were quiet until Scott pulled onto the freeway. "Craig," Elden said. "You can't imagine how grateful we are to have you drive us around."

"My pleasure."

Elden affected an accent. "We'd like to make you an offer you can't refuse."

"You sound more like an Englishman than the Godfather," Harriet laughed.

"Anyway, the two of us are too old to drive anymore. If you'd agree to take us where we need to go, we'd like to give you this car."

Scott was stunned. No one had ever given him anything like this. "You've got to be kidding."

"No, no, we're serious. This way, you'd have a way to get to work." Harriet interrupted, "When we found out about you being robbed, it worried us sick."

Scott remembered vaguely telling them about the robbery when he'd first moved in, but couldn't believe they'd remember it.

"Please, tell us you'll accept," Elden pleaded.

"I can't believe it," Scott said.

The conversation continued until they pulled into the driveway. Scott retrieved the walker from the trunk and helped Harriet from the car. When Elden was finally able to climb out of the back seat, Scott tried to hand him the keys, but the old man just shook his head and closed Scott's fist over them.

"Take good care of the old girl," Elden said with a wink.

A horn honked and Scott saw Charlie pull up to the curb.

CHAPTER 28

Monday, September 3, 1984

Craig, this is my Dad," Charlie said with a nod of his head. Mr. Rogers extended his hand and took Scott's.

"My son says you're a good worker." He fanned the charcoal. The briquettes were turning to a grey-white powder in the grill.

"I try to be."

"And this is my mom," Charlie said as a tall, rawboned woman came out of the house carrying a plate of hamburgers and hotdogs.

"Nice to meet you," Scott said.

She placed the plate next to the grill, wiped her hands on her apron, and shook Scott's hand. "Charlie has told us all about you," she said with a smile.

As much as he knows. "He's a good worker," Scott said. "We work well together."

The kitchen screen door opened and a beautiful young woman appeared carrying a platter of fruit. "Hey, sis," Charlie called to her. "Come meet my friend Craig."

Scott tried to keep from staring as the girl descended the stairs and placed the platter on the picnic table. She picked up a dish towel from the end of the table and wiped her hands as she joined Charlie and Scott.

"This is my little sister, Teresa," Charlie said with a smile. "This is my friend Craig."

Teresa's dark eyes seemed to light up as she smiled at Scott. "Pleased to meet you," she said.

Scott nodded his head. "Likewise." She took a step backward then headed back into the kitchen.

"She's a senior this year," Charlie said. "Smarter than a whip. Puts me to shame."

"She seems real nice," Scott said, trying to keep his voice neutral.

"Hamburger or hotdog?" Charlie's father called from the grill.

In the next ten minutes, as if by magic, a dozen of Charlie's relatives appeared. Scott was introduced to two uncles, two aunts, and a batch of cousins. After they finished eating, a game of horseshoes began. The others threw the metal shoes wildly at the iron pipes driven in the ground about forty feet apart near the back fence.

Scott had been sitting in the shade of a palo verde tree trying to find respite from the heat. He felt a hand on his shoulder. "Want to be my partner?" Teresa spoke from behind him.

Scott felt a tingle run down his spine. "Sure," he managed to say. The two of them moved to the horseshoe pit. Charlie and one of his cousins were their opponents. Neither team was very accomplished, and the match ended in a draw. When it was over, Scott moved back into the shade of the tree and Teresa followed him.

"Sorry if I let you down," he said with a shrug of his shoulders.

"Seems like both of us could use some practice," she replied with a little chuckle. They chatted for a few minutes before Charlie stepped over to them.

"Ready to go?" he asked.

"Sure," Scott pushed himself to his feet then turned and offered Teresa his hand. He pulled her up from the ground.

"Thanks." Scott started to follow Charlie across the lawn when Teresa called to him, "Will I see you again?"

Scott stopped in his tracks, turned around, and walked to her side. "I sure hope so. Would you like to go to a movie or something?"

"When?"

Scott quickly reviewed the week in his mind. With the holiday, he'd be working Tuesday through Friday. "How about Saturday?"

"What time?"

"I'll pick you up at six o'clock, okay?"

Teresa nodded her head. "Sounds good to me," she said with a smile.

Scott hurried to catch up with Charlie. *This has been one of the best days of my life.*

CHAPTER 29

Friday, October 12, 1984

Scott pulled the Road Runner into the Rogerses' driveway. He stepped out of the car and brushed a piece of lint from his brand new navy-blue, pinstripe suit. He had splurged $150—a week's pay—at Diamond's, but now owned a suit, a white shirt, and a tie.

He took a deep breath and climbed the stairs to the front porch. The doorbell chimed its deep-throated notes and a moment later, Mrs. Rogers opened the door. "Craig, you look handsome," she said. "Come in, Teresa will be ready in a minute or two. I'll go help her finish getting ready. Please, have a seat."

Scott stepped into the living room and took a seat on the over-stuffed couch. He had been here three times since Labor Day to pick up Teresa for movie dates, but this was the first time he'd had time to really inspect the room. A beautiful, serene landscape painting hung over the mantel. It showed a mountain lake and stream. Scott stood up and examined the painting. The name "Parker" appeared in the bottom right hand corner. *I wonder who that was?* Scott shook his head. *I know so little about so many things.*

He was still admiring the painting when he heard a sound behind him and turned around. Teresa stood in the archway dressed in a pale blue gown. Her dark chestnut hair had been drawn up into a chignon that was wrapped with a dark blue ribbon. "Hello, handsome," she said with a smile that lit up the room.

Scott swallowed. "You look amazing," he said.

Mrs. Rogers stepped into the room. "How late are you going to be?"

"I'll have her home before midnight," Scott said.

"Well, then you two have a good time. You make a handsome couple."

Scott led Teresa to the car, opened the door, and helped her to her seat. On the floor next to the stick shift was a corsage in a plastic box. Scott climbed into the car and picked up the container. "This is for you."

"Thank you. Will you pin it on me?"

With shaking hands, Scott pinned the corsage onto Teresa's dress, afraid he might stick her with the pin. "You look beautiful," he said nervously.

"You don't look so bad yourself, Craig." She slid a little closer to him on the seat.

Scott started the car and began backing out of the driveway. "I've made reservations at the Lunt Avenue Marble Club," he said. "I hope that's okay."

"Perfect," she said snuggling into the seat. "I appreciate you taking me to the homecoming dance."

"My pleasure," Scott said, meaning it.

He drove past the Arizona State University campus to Apache Boulevard and found a parking place near the restaurant. Scott helped Teresa out of the car, and she slipped her hand into his as they walked down the sidewalk. He felt tingles run up and down his spine.

After dinner, they drove to the high school and entered the gymnasium. The ceiling was festooned with crepe paper streamers, and potted shrubs had been placed strategically around the perimeter of the room. A five-piece band was playing slow dance music as they made their way onto the floor. Scott had never considered himself much of a dancer, but Teresa seemed able to follow even his clumsy footwork.

When the dance ended, Teresa took him by the hand and wove her way through the other dancers to a table that offered punch and cookies. Scott reached for a cup of punch and handed it to his date. As he reached for a second one, he heard a girl's voice.

"Teresa, you look stunning. Who is this hunk? Where has he been hiding?"

Scott turned around and saw a short, blond girl in a too-tight red dress standing next to Teresa.

"This is Craig Spillman," Teresa said with a smile. "Craig, this is Mandy Richards. We have biology together." Scott shook Mandy's hand.

"This is my date, Arnold Madsen," Mandy said. "Of course, you know him, don't you, Teresa?" Scott shook his hand as well. "Are you a senior? I don't remember seeing you before."

"No," Scott said, "I graduated last year."

"Oh, are you going to ASU?"

Scott felt a bit of panic welling up inside his stomach. "No, I'm taking a year off to decide what I want to do."

Teresa squeezed his hand. "He and my brother are good friends," she said. "Oh, listen, I think they're playing our song." She pulled Scott out onto the dance floor. "Mandy is the class gossip. If we'd stayed there any longer she'd have been asking for your address and phone number so she could do a little research on you." She snuggled against Scott's chest. "I don't think I need her trying to steal you away."

"She couldn't do that," Scott replied huskily. "She doesn't hold a candle to you."

They danced for a moment before Teresa said, "Where did you go to high school?"

Scott thought for a moment before saying, "In Utah." *This is getting complicated.*

CHAPTER 30

Tuesday, May 14, 1985

I'm glad you could come with us," Mr. Rogers said as he, his wife, and Charlie accompanied Teresa and Scott into the high school auditorium. The hall at North High School was filling fast. Teresa left them and moved to her assigned seat near the front row. The four of them found seats and settled in for the awards program.

The stage was decorated with red-and-blue panels and on the middle one was a mustang, the school's mascot. Several people were seated on the stage. One of them stood and walked to the podium. "Parents, students, and friends, I hope you feel welcome this evening. Before we begin the awards, let me say that we are extremely proud of the seniors who will be graduating this year. As principal, I have been amazed at the abilities of these young people to excel." He paused and opened a folder. "But you didn't come here to hear me pontificate. Let's get to the business at hand." He removed a sheaf of papers from the open folder. "Behind me you see the department heads who will present their awards. First is Mrs. Stauffer from the art department." He beckoned to a thin, dark-haired woman who was seated in the chair furthest to his right. "Would you please hold your applause until all of the students from each department have been recognized?"

Mrs. Stauffer was followed by several more department heads, culminating with the athletic director. Each of them recognized outstanding students from their particular fields. The audience applauded the achievements of the students. The temperature in the auditorium rose as the hour progressed until many of the people were fanning themselves with their programs. When the departmental awards had been given, the principal introduced the head counselor, Mr. Barton.

"It is my pleasure to announce the scholarships that have been awarded to quite a few of our senior students." Next to him on the stage was a table covered with envelopes. He picked up the first stack, "The following students have received a one thousand dollar scholarship toward tuition." He read the names of five students, who left their seats and climbed up onto the stage to receive their scholarships. Applause broke out from the assembled crowd.

Mr. Barton continued with the rest of the scholarships on the table until only one was left. "It is my extreme pleasure to award this final scholarship," he said with a broad smile. "Would Teresa Marie Rogers please join me on the stage? Teresa arose from her front row seat and walked slowly to Mr. Barton's side. He opened a large manila envelope and removed a certificate.

Scott sat up straighter in his seat. Mr. and Mrs. Rogers grasped each other's hands.

"It is with great satisfaction that I present to Miss Rogers a scholarship to Arizona State University. The scholarship covers tuition, books, and a stipend for living expenses. As long as Teresa keeps her grades up this is renewable for four years." He handed the certificate to Teresa and shook her hand. "I have no doubt she will keep this scholarship since she is a straight A student here at North."

Scott leapt to his feet and began applauding. The audience clapped their hands and many of them whistled loudly. Mr. and Mrs. Rogers shook their heads in disbelief. "I can't believe it," Mrs. Rogers said joyfully.

The event ended with the concert choir singing the school song.

CHAPTER 31

Saturday, June 7, 1986

Charlie straightened Scott's tie. "Lookin' sharp, old man." In the past two years, Scott and Charlie had proven to be such good workers that they had been promoted to shift supervisors. While Charlie now worked the day shift, Scott continued to work the night shift, which had grown to five additional workers as the company expanded.

More importantly to Scott, his relationship with Teresa had flowered. He had become a regular fixture around the Rogerses' home.

When fall semester began at ASU and Teresa entered college, Scott felt a twinge of jealousy, realizing that he had walked away from a similar scholarship two years before. Teresa kept her four point GPA intact through both semesters and had been recognized by ASU President Phillips as an outstanding freshman student.

Teresa had taken a job at a floral shop, and Scott's night shift meant that weekends were their only chance to be together. A few times they had gone to church together at the Baptist church Teresa's family attended. This week, Charlie had invited them to double date with him and his new girlfriend, Amanda.

Scott and Charlie were standing in the Rogerses' living room waiting for Teresa. "What do you know about *Hannah and Her Sisters?*" Charlie asked.

Scott shrugged his shoulders. "All I know is that Teresa really wanted to see it." He looked at himself in the mirror that hung over the couch and brushed imaginary lint from his shoulder.

"Yeah, Amanda says she's heard it's real good." He walked into the hallway. "Teresa, get a move on or we're gonna be late."

As if waiting for the invitation, Teresa scurried down the hallway. "Sorry." She linked her arm through Scott's. "I'm ready if you are."

After picking Amanda up from her house, they drove across town to McKellips Road and the Scottsdale 6 Drive-In. Teresa scooted over next to Scott and put her head on his shoulder while Charlie and Amanda snuggled in the back seat. It was after nine o'clock before it was dark enough to start the movie. When it ended, Scott drove back to Amanda's house. Scott climbed out of the car and pushed his seat forward so Charlie could unfold himself from the back seat. He led Amanda to her front porch.

Scott took advantage of being alone with Teresa to pull her toward him and kiss her. She slipped her arms around his neck and kissed him back. It was only when Charlie returned to the car that they broke their embrace. Before Scott could open his door, Charlie walked to the passenger's door, opened it, and slid into the front seat. "Looks like there's room for me," he said with a wink. When they arrived at the Rogerses' home, Charlie hopped out. "Don't stay out too late, sis," he said.

Scott and Teresa watched her brother amble up the sidewalk and enter the house before Scott enveloped Teresa in his arms and kissed her again. After a few minutes, he released his hold and reached into his pocket. "Teresa," he said huskily, "I have something to ask you."

Teresa put a little space between the two of them. "Okay."

Scott licked his lips nervously. "This isn't the most romantic spot," he began. "I really don't know how to do this."

"Do what?" she smiled coyly at him.

Taking a deep breath Scott blurted out, "Would you . . . I mean . . . is there any way you'd consider marrying me?"

Teresa paused for a second before she threw herself at him. "Of course!" she screamed. "Of course." She kissed him passionately.

When they finally pulled apart, Scott opened the box in his hand and removed the engagement ring. "It's not very big, but someday I'll get you one you deserve."

"It's perfect," she replied as she slipped the ring on her finger and tilted it back and forth trying to catch the refraction of her front porch light. She kissed him again. "Let's go tell my mom and dad," she gushed.

"It's after midnight," Scott replied. "Why don't we wait 'till tomorrow?" He felt a bit of panic.

Teresa nodded her head. "When are we getting married?" She giggled. "Have you thought that far ahead?"

"I thought we needed to decide that together," he replied.

Teresa kept moving her hand back and forth, looking at the ring. "School starts in August."

"That's only a couple of months away," he said, trying to sound reasonable.

"Good thing I work for a florist," she said. "We can probably get a discount on the flowers."

Scott thought of the money he'd been saving and could see it dissolving rapidly. "I thought we might just have a small, private wedding," he said softly.

Teresa smiled at him and kissed him again. "Well, I don't think my family will have huge numbers to invite; what about your family?"

Scott cringed inwardly. "I'm all alone. Of course there are some guys at work, but still, it ought to be small." He glanced at his watch. "I'd better get you in the house or your mother will have my hide." He opened the door and helped Teresa slip out under the steering wheel. They walked hand in hand up to the front porch where Scott kissed her one more time before she entered the house.

On the way back to his apartment, he suddenly realized he'd have to find another place to live; and if he moved away from Elden and Harriet Archibald's, he wondered if they'd still let him keep the

Road Runner. He pulled into the driveway. *Why have I made things so complicated?*

CHAPTER 32

Sunday, June 8, 1986

So you think you'd like to marry my daughter?" Mrs. Rogers said with a slight smile.

"Yes," Scott barely whispered. His hands were drenched in sweat at he sat on the couch in the Rogerses' front room. Teresa sat next to him with her hand on his knee. "If I can have your permission and if Teresa will have me." She squeezed his knee.

"Well, I can't answer for Teresa, but we'd be delighted to have you as a son-in-law." Mr. Rogers pushed himself up from his recliner and grabbed Scott's hand. "Welcome to the family."

"Thank you, sir."

Mrs. Rogers stood up and crossed the room, as Scott and Teresa both got to their feet, and hugged her daughter before she hugged Scott. "Well, Craig, it seems like we have some planning to do."

Teresa interjected, "Mom, school starts August 18."

Mrs. Rogers' eyes flew open. "You're thinking of getting married before school starts?"

"We just want a small wedding, Mom."

"But that's just two months away."

Mr. Rogers put his arm around Scott's shoulders. "Craig, how do your folks feel about this?"

"I don't have any folks, Mr. Rogers, they've both passed."

"I'm so sorry. I didn't know. Forgive me."

Scott nodded his head. "There's nothing to forgive." Panic began to swell within him.

"If you don't mind me asking, how long have they been gone?" Mrs. Rogers asked.

Scott swallowed before answering, "Just a few years."

"How did they die?"

Scott scrambled to come up with a plausible answer. "Car accident. A drunk driver was going the wrong way on the freeway and hit them head on."

Mrs. Rogers threw her arms around him and hugged him. "That must have been terrible." Tears ran down her cheeks. "Do you have any brothers or sisters?"

Scott was about to blurt out Jill's name, when he realized they'd want to know where she was and that could lead down an interesting path. "No, I was an only child."

Mr. Rogers turned his head away, "That must have been tough on you—having to plan the funeral and all."

Scott nodded his head. "It wasn't very pleasant. But you do what you have to do."

They stood awkwardly silent for a couple of minutes before Mrs. Rogers said, "So, you really want to get married before school starts in August. We'd better get busy." She hurried into the kitchen and returned with a pad of paper and a pencil. "Have you thought who you are going to have perform the ceremony?"

Teresa and Scott sank back down onto the couch. "Do you think Pastor Johnson would do it?" Teresa asked.

"Probably," her mother answered. "I can call him and ask. Are you planning to be married in the church?"

Scott began to feel a little uncomfortable. All through his growing up years, his parents had emphasized a temple marriage and even though he hadn't been attending church for the past two years, that notion was still stuck in his mind. He realized Teresa belonged to another church, but still there was a lingering thought that wouldn't leave his mind alone.

"Of course," Teresa said. "Mom, if you'd call him, I'd appreciate it."

Mrs. Rogers glanced at her watch. "Well, no time like the present. Services were over a couple of hours ago." She walked into the kitchen and called the church. "Pastor, this is Jean Rogers. I have some exciting news and a question for you."

Scott and Teresa sat holding hands while Mr. Rogers smiled at them from his recliner. After a few minutes, Mrs. Rogers came back into the living room. "He said he'd be delighted to perform the marriage. I went so far as to find out when he's available the first week in August. The church is booked on the weekend, but you can have the wedding on Tuesday the fifth or Wednesday the sixth, if that's okay with you." She looked at the two of them.

Teresa nodded. "No problem, Mom." She turned to Scott, "Either of those work for you?"

"Either one works, I guess."

"Let's go with Tuesday, Mom. What else do we need to worry about?"

Mrs. Rogers laughed. "Oh, just a couple of other things like a dress, a reception, food, bridesmaids. You know, just a few little things." She turned to Scott. "Have you thought about who you'd like to have as your best man?"

Scott shook his head. "I really hadn't thought about it." He felt like a deer in the headlights. Things were moving along at a pretty astounding pace. "I guess Charlie, if he'd agree to it."

"I think he'd be honored," Mr. Rogers said. "We'll ask him when he gets home from Amanda's. If that's all right?"

Two hours later, Mrs. Rogers was finishing putting together a wedding list, and she and Teresa had basically planned the refreshments for the reception. Pastor Johnson had been called again and the date had been set. Scott was just getting ready to leave when Charlie popped through the door.

"Charlie, I have something to ask you," Scott said.

"Shoot."

"I'm wondering if you'd consider being my best man."

Without missing a beat Charlie said, "Of course." He grabbed Scott in a bear hug. "Teresa showed me the ring this morning. Although what she sees in you I'll never know."

Teresa punched her brother on the shoulder. "Well, he's handsome, polite, and honest to the core. What else do you need?"

Scott felt his stomach tighten. *Honest to the core. Hardly.* On the way home, he wondered how and when he would tell Teresa the truth.

CHAPTER 33

Tuesday, August 5, 1986

The chapel was cool inside in contrast to the 110-degree temperature outside. With only Teresa's family and a few of Scott's coworkers, half the pews were empty. He and Charlie stood near the pulpit with Pastor Johnson. The organist had been playing a prelude, but at the nod of the pastor's head, she began playing "Here Comes the Bride," and the audience in unison turned to see Teresa and her father enter the back of the chapel and start walking toward Scott in measured steps. The congregation arose.

Scott inhaled sharply; Teresa looked beautiful in her white satin gown. Hundreds of seed pearls had been sewn in an intricate pattern covering the front of the dress. A veil covered Teresa's face, but Scott could see her smile beaming through it. She and her father reached the front of the church and Charlie and Mr. Rogers took their seats on the front row leaving Scott and Teresa facing each other in front of Pastor Johnson. They held hands as the pastor began.

"Friends, please be seated." He smiled at the young couple and offered a few words of advice before he turned his attention to Scott and said, "Repeat after me. 'I, Craig Spillman, take thee, Teresa Marie Rogers, to be my wedded wife.'" Scott repeated the words and felt tears coming to his eyes. Pastor Johnson continued, "For better, for worse, for richer, for poorer, in sickness and in health, to love and to cherish." Scott repeated the words.

"Till death do us part." Scott's heart leapt within his chest as he repeated the phrase. Something deep inside him stirred as unbidden thoughts of a temple marriage with its eternal significance bubbled to the surface.

"According to God's holy ordinance; and thereto I pledge myself to you."

When Scott had completed his vows, Pastor Johnson turned to Teresa and had her repeat the same words. When she had finished, Pastor Johnson smiled at the two of them. "Craig Spillman and Teresa Marie Rogers, I pronounce you husband and wife; you may now kiss the bride."

After a lingering kiss, the two of them hurried back down the aisle. Mr. Rogers and her two sisters had decorated the church recreation hall with bouquets of white-and-purple flowers and bunting that matched. Scott and Teresa were escorted to an archway on one side of the room and all of the guests greeted them. The only people Scott had invited were six of the other people he worked with and Elden and Harriet Archibald. He'd driven to their home and picked them up before he dressed for the ceremony. Mr. Rogers was going to drive them home after the reception.

Elden grasped Scott's hand in his. "Craig, you've done yourself proud. She's a might pretty young lady."

"Elden, I can't thank you enough for all you've done for me."

"Nonsense. I'm glad you're only living a couple of blocks from Harriet and me. I'm going to take you up on your offer to drive us places we need to go."

"You can count on it." Scott introduced the elderly couple to Teresa.

She beamed at the two of them. "You're the ones who gave Craig your car. I can't believe how generous you are."

Harriet leaned on her walker, "Pish pash, it's nothing. This old ruffian's too old to drive anyway and Craig drives us whenever we need him."

"Like we say, he's like the son we never had," Elden said with a wink as they continued on down the line.

When the last person had wished them well, the two of them stepped forward and began to dance as Whitney Houston's song, "The Greatest Love of All," filled the hall. "Happy?" Scott whispered in her ear.

"Oh, yes," she sighed back. Then, after a few moments she said, "The only thing that would have made this perfect was if your parents had been able to be here." Scott stiffened as a wave of remorse flooded his mind. "But I'm sure they're happy for us, even if it's from the other side."

Chapter 34

Monday, May 8, 1989

Scott entered the ASU Activity Center and looked for Section M. Teresa's parents stayed close behind him as they worked their way through the crowd. The commencement exercises were scheduled to begin in fifteen minutes. "That was quite a traffic jam," Mr. Rogers said.

"Yeah, we were lucky to find a parking place," Scott replied. "There's our section," he said as he pointed at a sign hanging over one of the portals.

They joined the queue of people streaming through the gateway into the arena. They were handed programs by a couple of young people who didn't look as if they were old enough to be in college; then they made their way to their seats. "I'm so proud of Teresa," her mother said. "She's the first person in our extended family to graduate from college."

Mr. Rogers turned toward Scott. "Craig, have you ever wished you'd gone to college?" He raised his hands as if he were halting an oncoming charge. "Not that you're not doing all right for yourself."

Scott shrugged his shoulders. "Yeah, sometimes I wished I'd have gone on to school." The recognition of his scholarship rattled in his brain. "But I'm pretty happy with CFI."

Duane patted him on the shoulder. "You've done well. I wish Charlie had stayed there, but I guess he's happy working for the phone company."

"I miss working with him. I think he'd be the assistant manager instead of me if he'd stayed."

Duane nodded his head. "Sometimes those little decisions we make in life produce big changes down the road."

Scott nodded his head. *If you only knew.*

At that moment, an organist began to play "Pomp and Circumstance," and a procession of graduating students entered the arena and proceeded to their seats. Scott looked for his wife, but everyone was dressed in similar caps and gowns, and it was hard to tell one from another. Suddenly, her mother spotted her.

"Look, she's just reached the row of chairs on the left," Mrs. Rogers said as she waved her hand.

Scott watched with pride and a little envy as Teresa slipped down the row and took her seat. Even from a distance he could see the maroon-and-gold tassel signifying summa cum laude. Except for an A- in a calculus class she had earned straight A's.

When all of the graduates were seated, the president of the university, J. Morton Phillips, stepped to the podium.

"This is quite a sight. I must say that in the years I have had the honor to be president of this fine university, I have never ceased to be amazed at the quality of students who attend here. My wife, Bonita, and I will sorely miss the association we have had with you." He continued to speak for several more minutes before he turned the microphone over to the other speakers on the program. Three of the graduating seniors spoke briefly and then Teresa took her place at the podium. Her speech was short and to the point as she thanked her professors, her parents, and her husband for all of the encouragement they had given her. She returned to her seat before the department chairs began inviting their graduates to approach the stand and receive their diplomas. As each name was read, applause and whistles erupted from the audience.

Teresa handed the card with her name on it to the man who was announcing the graduates. "Teresa Marie Rogers Spillman; graduating summa cum laude." She walked slowly across the stage to where her diploma was handed to her before Dr. Phillips shook her hand while they paused for a picture to be taken.

"Your speech was impressive, young lady," Dr. Phillips said. "Almost as impressive as your academic record."

"Thank you, sir."

The ceremony continued for almost another hour before the closing moments when tassels were moved from one side of the caps to the other. Then the recessional began. Scott and the Rogerses made their way out of the portal to the circular hallway that ran around the building. Teresa had told them to wait for her, and it was not long before she made her way through the crowd to their side.

Scott hugged her. "Congratulations, sweetheart."

"I couldn't have done it without you," she said as she kissed him.

Mr. Rogers spoke up, "Let's go celebrate. I've booked us a reservation at the Top of the Rock."

Scott's eyes flew open, "Isn't that pretty expensive?"

"Perhaps, but well worth it to celebrate Teresa's graduation." He opened the door of the arena and led the four of them down the steps. The Rogerses' new Chrysler Valiant was parked a block and a half from the activity center and the sidewalks were crowded, but before long they reached the car. Mr. Rogers unlocked the car and Scott and Teresa climbed into the back seat; a few minutes later, they were headed down University Avenue.

Mrs. Rogers turned in her seat. "Well, you're a college graduate now, honey, what's next?"

"I've been looking for a job,"

"I wouldn't think you'd have any trouble finding one," her mother said cheerfully. "Especially graduating with high honors."

"Mom, I'm not sure how many openings there are in Phoenix for oceanographers."

There was a moment of silence before her mother spoke again, "Does that mean you'll be moving? We've been so happy to have you living so close."

"I don't know, Mom. Scott's pretty happy with his job."

Scott slipped his arm around Teresa's shoulders. "We need to talk about that, I guess." With only a high school education, he was reluctant to leave the position he had; especially since he had been promoted at the start of the year.

"Well, I'm sure you'll make the right decision," Mr. Rogers said. "We're here. I hope everybody's hungry."

CHAPTER 35

WEDNESDAY, JUNE 28, 1989

Scott walked into the kitchen. He had just finished his shift. With the promotion he'd received, he was now working day shift, which was a major relief to him. He could smell something cooking on the stove and he lifted the lid and looked into the pot. A savory aroma engulfed him.

"Smells good," he said.

"You're home," Teresa called from the front room. "Dinner will be ready in ten minutes. I hope tacos are all right."

"Absolutely." He walked down the hallway to their bedroom, pulled off his sweat-soaked shirt, and dropped it in the laundry basket. He showered quickly and put on some clean clothes before walking back into the kitchen. Teresa was filling taco shells with the meat she'd simmered on the stove. He put his arms around her and kissed her. "How was your day?"

She picked up the plate of tacos and carried it to the tiny table. "Okay, I guess."

A few minutes later, they were eating dinner and Scott noticed Teresa was uncharacteristically quiet. "Have you heard anything from your brother?" Scott asked, trying to start some conversation.

Teresa shook her head. "Last time I talked to Mom, she said he and Amanda are thinking of moving again."

"Where to?"

Teresa shrugged her shoulders. "I don't know." She lapsed back into silence. When they finished eating, she cleared the table and put the dishes in the sink.

"I'll do those," Scott said as he started water running over the plates. Teresa nodded her head and walked into the living room. Once the dishes were done Scott joined her. "Is something wrong?" he asked.

Without saying a word, Teresa retrieved an envelope from the end table and handed it to her husband. It was addressed to Teresa and the return address said *Woods Hole Oceanographic Institute, Falmouth, Massachusetts.* Scott slipped the letter out of the envelope.

> *Dear Mrs. Spillman,*
>
> *We received your inquiry as to positions that might be open at Woods Hole. The Coastal Systems Group is currently seeking a Research Assistant to join their team. This is a full-time position and is eligible for benefits. The initial appointment will be for one year; however, I am pleased to tell you that after reviewing your academic record, the team expects this will become a tenured position for you.*
>
> *If you are interested in joining the WHOI team, please contact me as soon as possible. The team will begin their assignment August first.*

Scott finished reading the letter and noticed the salary was nearly twice what he was currently making. He looked at Teresa. "Are you seriously considering this?" he said quietly as he held the letter in front of him.

Teresa took a deep breath before nodding her head. "Craig, it's what I studied for. It's what I want to do." Her voice was barely a whisper.

He sat down heavily on the couch. "What about my job? Do you expect me to just pick up and go?" He shook his head slightly.

"Craig, I'm sure you can find work in Massachusetts." Her voice was soft and placating.

Scott was trying to contain himself. "Just when did you apply for this job? Why didn't you tell me?"

Teresa stood up and walked to the front window. She looked out at the sun-lit street in front of her. Her hands were crossed behind her back. "Craig, actually it was part of my college program. We all wrote letters to see if there were any positions open."

"I see." He relaxed. "So you don't really have to accept. I mean, it isn't a done deal, is it?"

She turned with tears in her eyes. "No, and if we say we're not moving, I'll write them and refuse the offer."

"But you really want to accept," he said with a slight sneer.

Teresa nodded her head. "Yes, I do, Craig. I just feel like I'm spinning my wheels and not using any of the knowledge and skill I learned at ASU." She returned to the couch and took his hand in hers. "But if you say 'no' I'll honor your decision."

Scott took a deep breath and exhaled slowly before answering, "Go ahead. I can't hold you back. I'll let them know at work that I'll be leaving." He put his arm around her. "How soon will we have to go? I suppose we'll need some time to find an apartment."

"I don't know. Maybe if we headed back to Massachusetts after the Fourth of July, we'd have time to get settled and I'd have time to get briefed on the project before we leave."

"Leave?"

"Didn't you see that we'd be sailing on August first and would be gone until about October thirty-first?"

Scott shook his head. "I guess I didn't read it that closely. You'd be gone for three months?"

Teresa nodded her head. "That's the way these research projects go. We'd be on the ship gathering data for three months and then spend the rest of the year analyzing what we've collected."

Scott shook his head. "I guess that will give me time to find a job and learn to take care of myself."

"Craig, you were doing a pretty good job of taking care of your-self before we met. You'll be just fine." She kissed him. "Thank you, sweetheart." She stood up. "I'm sure this is going to be a great move for us. Now I've got a harder task. I've got to tell my mother we're leaving."

CHAPTER 36

Tuesday, October 24, 1989

I'll bet you're happy she'll be home next week," Charlie Rogers said.

"Absolutely. It's been a long three months. At least you and Amanda are only a couple of hours away."

Charlie stretched. "Yup, we can make it from Boston to Mashpee and back on half a tank of gas." They were standing in the front yard of Scott's apartment on Falmouth Road.

"It's great to be here," Scott said. "We're less than half an hour from Woods Hole and only about ten minutes from the marine shop where I work."

"Man, you came out of that smelling like a rose. Who'd a thought you'd show up here the first day they were looking for a manager. Some guys have all the luck."

"Well, you're doing okay yourself, Charlie."

Charlie smiled. "I guess. Probably the smartest thing I ever did was trick Amanda into marrying me. It made finding a job out here pretty easy when her uncle runs that fleet of trucks out of Boston."

"I'm not sure it was much of a trick. I think she was the one trying to convince you to marry her."

"Maybe. Anyway, I've got to get on the road." He started walking down the sidewalk toward the semitruck that sat idling at the curb. "Let's get together when Teresa's back in port. Okay?"

Scott saluted. "Absolutely. Either you and Amanda can come down here or we'll drive up to Boston."

Charlie climbed into the cab of the truck, tooted the air horn, and pulled on down the street. Scott waved, then opened the mailbox and retrieved a half dozen letters. He sorted through them as he walked into their apartment. Nestled among the credit card offers was an envelope addressed to him. The return address showed *Mangum, Morgan, and Flowers, Sacramento, California.* Scott slit it open and withdrew the note inside.

Mr. Spillman,

Let me introduce myself. My name is LeRoy Flowers of the law firm of Mangum, Morgan, and Flowers. We represent the estate of the late Mary Lois Hancock Spillman, who died March nineteenth of last year. In her will, which has not been updated in nearly twenty years, she left all of her estate to her son, Craig. We have been in the process of settling her estate for the past several months.

We were under the impression that Craig had passed away prior to his mother's passing; however, in doing due diligence, we discovered that you, Craig Spillman, are living. There seems to be some confusion since it appears there is a Craig Spillman buried in the family plot in Sacramento, but five years ago a Craig Spillman, who purported to be the son of Justin and Mary Lois Spillman applied for a social security account and driver's license.

If, indeed, you are the son of Mary Lois Spillman, would you please contact us immediately with corroborating evidence of your identity. While I am not at liberty to discuss the specifics of the estate, it is sufficient to say it is substantial.

If you are not the person in question, would you please contact us in order to clear up this matter?

Thank you,

LeRoy Flowers

Scott's heart began beating furiously in his chest. *If they can track me down, so can my father.* It became more and more obvious that either way he responded he was in trouble. For a moment, he considered trying to bluff his way through the situation and claim to be the missing son; especially with a substantial settlement; but he realized that he could not provide any proof that he was Craig Spillman, and if he did, he would obviously be guilty of fraud. On the other hand, if he contacted them and said he was not the person they sought, would this law firm pursue legal action since he clearly had assumed Craig Spillman's name? What was the penalty for pretending to be someone else? The more he thought about the conundrum the more frantic he became. He set the letter down on the kitchen counter while he considered his options.

He left the house and began wandering the streets. The sun was setting, and the evening chill finally drove him back to their apartment. As he approached the front door, he saw a light on in the living room. He opened the door and saw his wife sitting on the couch with the letter in her hands.

"What does this mean?" she said.

"What are you doing home?" he replied. His emotions ran between joy at seeing his wife for the first time in nearly three months, and the panic of seeing the letter in her hand.

"We finished a week early. I thought I'd surprise you. Obviously, I did." She stood up from the couch. "I thought you said your mother was dead when we got married."

Scott felt beads of sweat gathering on his forehead. "She was, I mean, she is."

"What's going on here, Craig?"

Scott wiped his face with his hand. "Teresa, it's just a mix up; somebody else with the same name."

"And parents with the same name?" she looked skeptically at him. "Come on, what's going on here?"

With a huge sigh, Scott sank onto the couch. "It's a long story." He tried to take his wife's hand in his, but she pulled it away. "One I should have told you a long time ago."

"It better be good," she replied.

CHAPTER 37

Thursday, October 26, 1989

Scott loaded his suitcase into the trunk of the Road Runner. He thought back to two nights ago when he'd finished telling Teresa the whole story. She sat immovable on the couch. When he'd tried to touch her, she'd pulled away and stared at him with glacial eyes.

"It's all a lie," she said. "Our whole life together is a lie. How could you do this, Craig? Or should I call you Scott?"

"I'm sorry," he blurted out. "I still love you, Teresa, with all my heart."

She turned away from him. "You have a funny way of showing it. I can't believe you'd do this. Are we even married?"

No matter how he'd begged her to forgive him, she had rebuffed everything he said.

Nothing had improved the next morning, and Teresa left for Woods Hole without a word. Last night she had not returned home. When he called her number at work, she refused to talk to him. Scott packed his belongings and hoped that if he left for a few days they'd be able to smooth things over. He'd told his boss at the marine shop he'd be gone for an indefinite time. Just as he was leaving, the phone rang. "Hello."

"Hello, is this Scott Simms?"

Scott almost dropped the receiver. "Yes," he said tentatively. "Who's this?"

"My name is Sheldon Fields. I'm an attorney and I've been retained by your wife to initiate divorce proceedings . . ."

Before anything more could be said, Scott dropped the phone back on the cradle, ran out of the house, and drove away. He had no idea where he was going, but he knew his welcome in Massachusetts had just run out. He filled his car up with gas and headed to I-90. By late afternoon, he'd passed through Albany and followed the shores of Lake Erie to Buffalo. All day long he'd racked his brain trying to think of somewhere that would allow him to hide. He had no idea what action Teresa would take besides the divorce, nor did he know exactly what he was guilty of, but he was sure that that phase of his life was over.

"How could I have been so stupid?" he muttered as he slammed his hands on the steering wheel. He found a cheap motel and spent a restless night trying to come to grips with the situation he found himself in. But no solution immediately surfaced. He tried calling Teresa again, but all she said was, "It's over." The next morning, he continued on through Cleveland toward Indiana. As he began passing by little towns, he wrestled with whether it would be easier to hide in an obscure village or in a big city.

He left the freeway outside of Gary and took country roads, looking for a place to settle. Eventually, he reached the banks of the Mississippi and crossed over to the west side in Burlington, Iowa. Scott stopped for dinner before taking the road that paralleled the Mississippi. Less than half an hour later he entered the sleepy little town of Keokuk. He pulled into a motel and tried to settle down for the night, but sleep wouldn't come. He tossed and turned as he thought of everything he was leaving behind. Not only was he fleeing from Teresa, but he'd also miss his friendship with her brother. *What a mess I've made of my life,* he thought.

When morning came, he dragged himself out of bed, showered, and walked a couple of blocks to a diner where he ordered breakfast.

Four elderly men were seated in the booth behind him and Scott couldn't help but overhear their conversation. "I guess that kid Larry hired took off night before last. Emptied the till first."

"Always thought there was somethin' strange about that kid."

"Getting harder and harder to hire honest labor."

Back and forth the conversation bounced until one of the men drained his coffee cup and struggled to his feet. "See you gents later." He started out the door and Scott caught up to him.

"I wasn't eavesdropping, but I couldn't help but hear what you were saying."

The old man looked at Scott through rheumy eyes. "You're new around here, ain't cha?"

Scott nodded his head. "Just moved into town and I'm looking for a job." He extended his hand and old man shook it. "I heard you say Larry might be looking for someone."

The old man removed his well-worn cap and scratched the sparse hairs that flew unfettered from his head. "Maybe, but I think he's a little gun shy after that last kid ran out on him."

Scott nodded his head. "I understand." He paused a moment before asking, "Just what kind of work does Larry do?"

"He runs that auto parts store down the street. You know anything about auto parts?"

Scott smiled broadly. "I've spent five years working at a warehouse that handled all sorts of parts. I'm sure I'd be a quick learner."

The old man replaced his cap and considered Scott for a minute or two. "Well, I guess Larry will have to decide. I ain't hiring anybody for him." He pointed further down the street. "His place is on the other side of Main Street. See, where that red-and-green sign is."

"Thanks, I hope I see you around town." He hurried back to the motel, climbed in the Road Runner, and headed down the street. Half an hour later he had a job working for Larry.

CHAPTER 38

Friday, June 29, 2007

arry, I'm sorry it has come to this." Scott brushed his hair out of his eyes and sat down heavily on the stool behind the counter. "I wish you'd reconsider."

"Can't do it. With two national chains in town, I just don't get enough business to survive. Besides, I'm nearly seventy years of age and it's time for me to retire and spend more time with my wife." Larry patted Scott on the shoulder. "My only regret is having to let you go. You've been a hard worker, Craig. You've pulled more than your share of the load in all the years you've worked here."

"I've tried." Scott shifted on the uncomfortable stool. "You've been great to work for, Larry. I hope this doesn't mean we'll never see each other again."

"Keokuk's too small for that." Larry took a deep breath and gazed out the front window of his shop. He fought to keep the tears from spilling down his cheeks. "Course, Betts wants to take a cruise. So I guess we'll be heading down to Puerto Vallarta next week."

Scott stood up and put his hands on Larry's shoulders. "You have a good time, my friend; you deserve it."

Larry nodded his head. "What are you going to do, Craig?"

"Well, there aren't many jobs available in Keokuk, but I hear Walmart is hiring. I think I'll give them a try. I really like it here."

Larry shook his head slightly. "I can't believe how riled up people were about them building that big store. A lot of the old timers, like me, thought they'd never have enough customers to make a go of it. But look at how full the parking lot is all the time."

"Yeah, I think they're doing all right."

"Well, if that's what you want to do, I hope they hire you. You're a good worker. Want me to write you a letter of recommendation?"

"That's not necessary, but if it's okay I'll put you down as a reference."

"I'd be pleased." He walked around the counter and took a long, last look around his shop. "Brings back a lot of good memories," he muttered. Resolutely, he walked to the front door and opened it. "I guess there's no use in delaying things." He waited for Scott to exit. "How are things going with you and the Simpson gal?"

"Okay," Scott said with a smile. "She seems to be able to put up with me."

Larry chuckled. "She's a keeper, that one. I don't know why somebody hasn't snatched her up before this." He looked expectantly at Scott. "You planning to marry her?"

Scott shrugged his shoulders. "I don't know. I'm pretty old to be getting married."

Larry snuffled, "Craig, you're not that old. But you're getting older every day." He winked at Scott. "You know not making a decision means you've made a decision, if you know what I mean. She's not going to wait for you forever." He closed the door, produced a key, and locked it. "Well, I guess I'll be going. Thanks for everything." He climbed into his car and pulled out of the parking lot.

Scott walked to his pickup truck and settled down into the seat. *What in the world can I do? I'm sure Teresa divorced me, but I've never checked because I knew it would tell them where I am.* He clutched the steering wheel with both hands. *Ah, Teresa.* He felt tears forming in his eyes and he brushed them away with the back of his hand. *But what if we're still married—if we ever were.* He shook his head as he remembered the woman he'd left behind.

For the last three years, he'd been dating Charese Simpson on and off. She was a couple of years younger than he was and extremely attractive. Still, nothing had really sparked between them. They seemed comfortable in their dating relationship. They'd go to a movie or dinner once or twice a week, but somehow he couldn't shake his memories of Teresa; and he was worried about committing the same mistake again—Charese only knew him as Craig Spillman.

He started the Ford and backed out of the parking lot with one last look at the shop where he'd worked for the last eighteen years. In that time he'd become well entrenched in Keokuk and had explored the area around until he felt at home. The only concern he had was the missionaries from Nauvoo on the other side of the river. There were a lot of older couples who served there and he was afraid there might be someone from his hometown of Bountiful, Utah. Fortunately, few of them ever came to Larry's shop and after a while he relaxed. He'd grown a beard, which he kept neatly trimmed, and he'd let his crew cut grow until he'd be hard to recognize.

Scott pulled into the Walmart parking lot and went into the customer service area. The manager was a man that Scott had helped several times solving problems with his vintage Chevrolet. "Craig, how are you?" Bill Lowder, the manager, said.

"Okay, I guess."

"I heard Larry was finally closing down. That's sad."

Scott nodded his head. "That's why I'm here. Are you hiring?"

Bill stepped behind the counter, opened a drawer, and pulled out an application. "Fill this out, Craig. We always have someone coming or going."

Scott took the application and turned to go when Bill said, "Matter of fact, do you know the Wheeler kid?" Scott shook his head. "He's a Mormon. He's going on a mission for his church. He'll be leaving in a couple of weeks. If you want, you can fill in for him."

Scott blinked his eyes. "That would be great. When do you want me to come?"

Bill looked at the calendar on the wall. "Let's see, his last day is Friday, the sixth. What if you come in on the fifth and I'll have you shadow him for a day, then you can start the next day?"

"You think one day will do it?"

"Yeah, I've watched you work down at Larry's. You impress me as a pretty bright guy. I think you'll pick it up pretty fast."

Scott shook Bill's hand. "Thanks, you won't be sorry."

"I'm sure I won't. Now finish filling out that application so we can make it official."

CHAPTER 39

Wednesday, August 1, 2007

Charese Simpson accepted Scott's help as she climbed up into the seat of his truck. "Thanks, Craig," she said with a bright smile.

Scott nodded his head, hurried around the front of the Ford and climbed into the driver's seat. "I thought we'd drive up to Fort Madison and have dinner at the Palms, if that's okay with you."

"Sounds wonderful."

The thirty-minute drive was pleasant. The unusually hot weather of the past week had broken and the humidity had dropped as well. Scott pulled into the parking lot and helped Charese out of the truck. No sooner did they enter than the manager greeted them as if they were long-lost friends. He showed them to a table and sat down next to Scott. "You've got to try the green beans," he said. "They are superb."

Charese picked up the menu and began perusing it.

"I'll give you a minute," the manager said as he slid out of the booth.

"What's this about the beans?" she asked.

Scott shook his head. "I don't know. I don't come here that often."

Charese smiled across the table. "It must have been with one of your other women folk; it's the first time I've ever been here."

Scott blushed. "Nope, just a couple of times Larry and his wife invited me. I think they felt sorry for me, you know. The manager always acts like that, he's kind of an odd duck, but the food's great." She reached across the table and took his hand in hers. "That's good to know; even though I'm not much of a jealous woman."

At that moment, a waiter appeared to take their order. Reluctantly, Scott released Charese's hand. While they waited for their food to be delivered, Charese asked, "How's the new job, Craig?"

"Good. The people I work with seem happy. There's not a lot of complaining."

"So you're planning on staying?" She smiled broadly. Her face was glowing in the candlelight. She looked extremely alluring.

"Yup." He cleared his throat and licked his lips. He swiveled his head to see if anyone was paying any attention to them before he said, "Charese, we've been dating for three years."

She nodded her head. "Has it been that long?"

"Yes. I hope you won't be offended if I ask you something."

"Oh, I don't get easily offended. What do you want to ask, Craig?"

Scott licked his lips again. "Where do you see our relationship going?"

She smiled coyly. "Well, that's up to you, I think, Craig. Where do you want it to go?"

He looked into her eyes while he summoned his courage. "Charese, we're not spring chickens—please don't take offense at that—and I think we're past the teenage hormone rushes. At least I think we are." He took a deep breath. "Anyway, is there any way you'd consider marrying me?"

Her eyes lit up. "Why, Craig, I do believe you're proposing. Am I right?"

He nodded his head. "Yes, I guess I am."

"And just how soon do you plan for us to get married?"

"I guess that's up to you," he fumbled.

The waiter appeared. "The Steak-al-Arabia?"

Scott gestured at Charese. "That's for the lady."

He placed the plate in front of Charese. "Then the Coconut Shrimp must be for you." Scott nodded his head. "Enjoy."

They ate in silence for several minutes before Charese said, "I've always wanted a Christmas wedding."

Scott finished swallowing the food in his mouth. "Sounds good to me."

Charese sucked her lower lip into her mouth and nibbled on it. "But there's a slight problem."

Scott's forehead knitted, "What kind of problem?"

She took a deep breath and exhaled slowly. "You might want to reconsider after I . . ." She stopped.

Scott sat up straight. "What?"

"I'm still married to my first husband."

"You're what?" Scott nearly dropped his fork.

Charese lowered her eyes. "We've been separated for nearly twenty years. I guess neither one of us went to the trouble of filing for divorce."

Scott's mind flashed back to when he and Teresa had parted. He assumed she'd finished filing for divorce, but he really didn't know that for sure.

"I don't know how long it takes for a divorce to be final in Iowa." She looked into Scott's eyes for understanding. "And to be honest, I don't know where Rob is. We were living in New Jersey when we separated. I haven't had any contact with him in at least ten years."

Scott sat dumbfounded. At last he broke the silence, "Well, will you find out? I mean, let's find out what the law says. Maybe after all that time . . . I mean, maybe it's like common-law marriage. Common-law divorce." He was stumbling over his words.

"I'll try to find Rob tomorrow and see what we need to do. I suppose I'd better find an attorney, or at least find out what I have to do to file for divorce. I'm sure it won't be a problem. I guess I just didn't think I'd ever want to get married again."

Scott reached across the table and took her hand in his. "And are you sure you want to now?"

She squeezed his hand. "Of course." She shrank back in her seat. "If you still want to. I mean, this has to be a shock."

"It is, but I understand more than you know."

"Really? I should have told you, but I didn't know if you were serious about our relationship."

They finished eating in silence and then walked out to Scott's truck. He helped Charese into the passenger seat before climbing in behind the wheel. She slid across the seat and he turned and kissed her. "Let's not set a date until we do a little investigating. Okay?"

"It will all work out," she said. "You've made me a very happy woman."

Scott kissed her again. As he started the truck he thought, *Maybe I need to do a little investigating of my own.*

CHAPTER 40

Friday, December 21, 2007

Charese had dressed carefully in an ecru gown with an empire waist. A white shawl covered her shoulders. Three weeks earlier, Scott had driven to Burlington and purchased a navy blue pinstriped suit. They drove up the river road to the Lee County courthouse in Fort Madison in Scott's Ford pickup.

"I'm getting my wish—a Christmas wedding," she said happily.

"I'm just glad your ex was so easy to work with. That was one of the quickest, easiest divorces I've ever heard of," he replied.

Charese shrugged her shoulders. "I'm not even sure he knew whether I was alive or dead. It must have been quite a shock hearing from me after all those years. Thank heaven for Google; he wasn't that hard to find."

"Even so, I'm happy he was so agreeable."

"So am I. And I'm glad we didn't make any firm plans until the divorce decree arrived." She put her hand on Scott's leg. "I've never been happier in my life. You're such a good man, Craig."

I wish I'd had some way of contacting Teresa without letting her know where I am. But certainly after all these years she's divorced me. He shuddered slightly, *if we were ever really married.*

They pulled into a parking place in front of the courthouse with its four impressive white pillars. "Well, here we go," he said as he slid out of his seat. "Ready to take this giant step?" He helped Charese out of the truck.

She nodded her head and linked her arm through Scott's. Together they climbed the steps toward the porch in front of the building. Evergreen wreaths were hung on either side of the doors and garlands encircled the pillars in Christmas finery. The previous week they'd driven to the courthouse, paid the fee for their marriage license, and arranged for a judge to perform the marriage. They'd agreed to a small, private ceremony. However, as they opened the door, they were surprised to see his old boss Larry and his wife, Betts, standing in the hallway along with a dozen of Scott's coworkers and a half dozen of Charese's friends from work. A cheer went up as the two of them entered the building.

A few minutes later. Judge Danielson came out of her office and invited the group into a conference room. She invited Scott and Charese to stand in front of her while she recited the wedding ceremony. At the conclusion, Scott slipped a ring onto Charese's finger and kissed his bride.

"May the rest of your lives be as happy as this day," Judge Danielson said as she hugged each of them. Immediately, the friends who had come to the wedding engulfed them. When they could escape, they ran out of the building and drove away.

"I wish we could go on a honeymoon," Scott said as they continued down the road, "But this is such a busy time of year; I was lucky Bill let me have the weekend off."

Charese snuggled close to him. "Next summer, when you have some vacation time, we'll get away for a few days. I'm just glad we didn't wait any longer." She kissed his cheek. "You've made me so happy, Craig." She held up her hand and looked at the ring. "Charese Spillman. That has a nice ring to it, don't you think?"

A slight shiver ran down Scott's spine.

CHAPTER 41

Monday, September 15, 2008

Scott finished filing the paperwork he'd been inspecting when Ruth Perkins, one of his service clerks, stuck her head into his office. "Craig, can you help this gentleman?"

Scott came out of his office to see an elderly couple standing near the counter. The man was dressed in a dark suit and white shirt and sported the telltale black tag of a missionary on his pocket. His wife was dressed nicely and had a similar missionary tag on her dress.

"What can I do to help you?" Scott asked. He looked closely at their name tags—*Elder and Sister Hatch.*

Elder Hatch had a folded up newspaper in his hand. He placed it on the counter and spread it out. "We're wondering if you carry anything similar to this," he pointed at an advertisement for a health food supplement.

Scott turned the newspaper around and looked closely at the ad. "We don't carry that specific brand, but I do believe we have something similar. Why don't you follow me and I'll show you what we have."

He slipped out from behind the counter and led the couple to the shelves near the pharmacy. He took a bottle from a shelf and handed it to the woman, who slipped a pair of reading glasses from her purse, put them on, and read the label. "Yes," she said with a slight nod of her head. "These will do."

Elder Hatch shook Scott's hand. "Thank you for being so helpful." The man smiled broadly at him before he and his wife made their way to a checkout counter.

Scott returned to his office. The newspaper Elder Hatch had brought was still on the counter. He picked it up and carried it back to his desk. He refolded the paper so that the front page was on top and noticed it was *The Davis County Clipper*. He blinked his eyes. *What a coincidence—a paper from my hometown.* He read the articles on the front page. It appeared that many of the issues they had been dealing with when he'd left were still being dealt with today. He even recognized some of the names in the stories. He felt a wave of nostalgia. On an inside page was the information on how to subscribe and on a whim, Scott took out a sheet of paper, wrote a letter to the *Clipper*, placed it an envelope, and enclosed a check. He had the paper mailed to Craig Spillman at Walmart rather than home, just to avoid any embarrassing questions.

In the year and a half he'd been working at Walmart, Scott had advanced very quickly. Bill Lowder had made him an assistant manager after only six months. Scott was an anomaly; he was younger than some of the cashiers, and older than all of the stock boys. He'd quickly made friends with all of the other employees, many of whom remembered him from the years he worked at Larry's. He was liked by everyone, and no one seemed particularly bothered by his promotion.

He was analyzing an order form as the store prepared for Christmas when his wife poked her head into his office. "Hey, good lookin' got time for a visit?" she said with a wink.

"Always time for you," he replied as she walked to his side and bent to kiss him. "What's up?"

"Just heading home and I thought I'd drop by."

"How was your day?" he asked.

"Pretty boring. Doc Harvey had to run over to Nauvoo to see about someone who thought he'd broken his thumb. So I just held down the office all afternoon." She pulled a chair over to his desk and sat down. "Ever been there?"

"Where?"

"Nauvoo. I went there when I first moved to Keokuk. They do some really interesting musicals."

Scott nodded his head. "Same with me. When I first moved into town, I did a little exploring and I saw a couple of the shows the missionaries do in Nauvoo. I haven't been back in years."

"Maybe we could go back over some time."

Scott shrugged his shoulders. "Sure, if you'd like."

Charese saw the *Clipper* on the corner of Scott's desk. "Where did that come from?" she asked.

Scott licked his lips. "A couple left it. I helped them find an herbal supplement and they forgot to take their paper with them."

She picked it up and flipped through a few pages. "Davis County? I've never heard of the place."

"It's just north of Salt Lake City," he replied.

"I've never been anywhere west of Iowa. Maybe we could take a vacation trip out west someday."

Scott nodded his head. "Maybe."

Charese leaned over and kissed him. "Well, I'm headed home. Don't be too late. I've got steaks for dinner." She stood up and winked over her shoulder as she left his office.

Chapter 42

That was really interesting," Charese bubbled as they walked across the new mown grass toward the parking lot. "The pageant was really tear jerking." She squeezed Scott's hand. "I don't know much about the Mormons. Of course I've heard about Brigham Young, but I didn't know much about Joseph Smith. What did you think about it?"

"It was very well done," he said carefully.

"Craig, we've never talked much about religion. I used to go to church when I was a little girl—my mother made me. But I haven't attended in years."

"Neither have I," he admitted. "What denomination were you?"

"It was kind of a non-denominational protestant church. I haven't thought about it in years. My mother sang in the choir. I think she really liked wearing a robe and standing up in front of the congregation. She liked being in the spotlight."

"What about your dad?"

Charese let go of Scott's hand and turned to face him with a look of concern on her face. "Craig, we've been married a year and a half and we've never talked much about our families at all. It's almost as if we've been avoiding them."

"I guess."

"Well, I think it's about time you learned about my family. Didn't you wonder why no one came to our wedding? Of course none of your family came either."

Scott squirmed a little as he unlocked the door of his truck and helped Charese into her seat. "Well, none of my family is alive," he said as he slid in under the steering wheel. "My mother and father are both dead." Outside the truck a cluster of fireflies blinked on and off.

Charese folded her hands in her lap. "When did they die?"

"Years ago," he replied. "Automobile accident."

Scott pulled out of the parking area and drove south toward Hamilton. "Craig, I think my mother is still alive. I haven't talked to her in years. She left me with my grandmother when she decided to chase her dream."

Scott glanced at Charese. "What was her dream?"

"I think it came in the form of little white powder that she sniffed up her nose." She lowered her head. "My grandmother used to hear from her every once in awhile, but when Grandma died, my mother didn't even come to the funeral."

"How old were you?"

"I was nine years old when my mother left, and I'd just turned sixteen when Grandma died."

"That must have been tough."

Charese nodded her head. "She was the only person who cared about me." She wiped a tear from her cheek. "So I helped bury Grandma—she had a sister who was still alive and offered me a place to live, but I just couldn't do it. I'd only seen her twice in my life."

"So what did you do?"

"I married Rob," she said softly.

Scott shifted in his seat. "How did you know him?"

"I was a car hop at a drive-in and he was a regular customer." She shook her head. "I started working there when I was fifteen. I'm not sure how Rob knew my grandmother had died, but a couple of days after her funeral he pulled in and told me he was sorry. We dated for a couple of months and then we got married."

"Just like that?"

Charese nodded her head. "It was a mistake. I know that now, but at the time I was struggling to find some direction in my life and Rob provided an answer."

Scott nodded his head. "I can see that." They drove into Hamilton and turned to take the bridge that crossed the Mississippi and took them home. "So how long did it last?"

"About a year." She shook her head again. "Then Rob enlisted in the army. He thought it was a ticket to getting a college education, but after basic training he was shipped out to the Persian Gulf."

"And you were left alone again."

Charese nodded her head. "So I graduated from high school and started college to become a nurse. At first we wrote each other every couple of days; then it dropped off until it was only once a month." She shrugged her shoulders. "Rob liked the military and I had almost graduated with my nursing degree."

"He must have been gone quite a while."

"Oh, he finished his tour and signed up for another go around. That's when we agreed to a separation and I took a job at Beaumont Hospital in Dearborn."

"So that was twenty years ago?"

"Well, we split about twenty years ago, but I went to work in Dearborn about fifteen years ago."

"So why did you decide to move to Keokuk?"

"Working in a hospital seemed kind of impersonal, and I heard from a friend who had moved to Keokuk that Dr. Harvey's nurse was retiring and that he'd need someone to replace her. So here I am. End of story."

"Thanks for sharing," Scott said softly. "But you haven't told me about your father."

"I never knew him. He and my mom split when I was about eighteen months old. She told me she was so mad at him that she tore up the only picture she had of him. And she refused to even mention his name. Kind of sad, isn't it? You get mad at someone and it changes the whole course of your life."

"I guess."

Scott turned off Main Street on Eighteenth Street and then onto Timea Street and their house. He helped Charese out of the truck and up the steps to the porch.

"Now you know my story, Craig, but I still haven't heard anything about yours."

Scott unlocked the door and entered the house. "Not much to tell. I was born in Sacramento and my folks died and are buried there."

Charese looked confused. "But I thought you said you were from Utah?"

"Oh, well, I moved there after my parents died." Scott tried to remember what story he'd told Charese about his past.

Charese sat down on the couch. "Okay, so what brought you to Keokuk?"

Scott shrugged his shoulders. "After my folks died, I just started looking for some place to settle down. I travelled quite a bit for a few years but when I drove into Keokuk, it felt like home."

Charese had been watching Scott closely. "What's the matter, Craig? You seem bothered about something. I've never seen you so jumpy."

Scott took a deep breath and tried to calm himself. "Bad memories, I guess."

"Like what?" A note of suspicion had crept into her voice.

"I don't know—jobs that weren't very fulfilling, friends that let me down. You know, just chasing my own rainbow, I guess."

Charese continued to stare at him. "What about other women, Craig? It's hard to believe you never settled down long enough to marry."

Scott felt as if an icicle ran down his spine. "I never had time, I guess; never stayed that long in one spot, until I met you." He started walking toward their bedroom. "I think it's time for bed. I have to get up early in the morning." *What's the matter with me? She bared her soul and I just lied to her.*

CHAPTER 43

Monday, December 21, 2009

Scott opened the kitchen door and stepped into the house. He had a bunch of red roses in his hand. "Charese," he called out. A moment later she came into the kitchen. "Happy anniversary," he said as he handed her the flowers.

"Oh, Craig, how thoughtful," she said as she threw her arms around him.

"How about going out to dinner?"

"You don't have to ask me twice," she said.

Scott kissed his wife before heading down the hallway toward their bedroom. "Let me take a quick shower and I'll be ready to go."

Charese followed him into the bedroom. "I'd better slip into something nicer too."

Twenty minutes later, they drove down the street to Angelini's Pizza. They'd discovered this pizza place when it expanded from take out only and now provided seating. Charese reached for Scott's hand.

"I have some news," she began.

"Oh?"

"It appears I'm going to have to look for a new job. Doc Harvey's retiring at the end of the year."

"Really? I thought he'd keep practicing until the day he died."

"Well, you thought that about Larry when you worked for him, and look what's happened with him."

Scott nodded his head. "So what are you thinking?"

"I guess there's an opening at the hospital."

"I thought you didn't like hospitals—you felt they were too impersonal."

She nodded her head. "Dr. Strope in Hamilton is looking for someone. Maybe that would be a better fit for me."

"Whatever you want."

Their food arrived and they ate silently for several minutes before Charese spoke again. "Craig, didn't you tell me your parents' names were Justin and Mary Lois?"

A shiver ran down his back. "Yes. Why?"

"I hope you don't think I was sneaking around or anything, but while I had some spare time this afternoon, I googled them."

"Oh, really. What did you discover?"

Charese looked into his eyes with a trouble look on her face. "Just as you said they were both dead and buried in Sacramento."

Scott nodded his head. "Like I said."

"But so was their son Craig. In fact, he's buried between his mother and father."

Scott tried to make light of her discovery. "Imagine the coincidence of two guys with the same name having parents with the same names."

"Craig. They are the only two people with those names buried in California." She waited for an explanation.

Scott stared at the tablecloth in front of him. "Oh," he finally said in a voice barely above a whisper.

The waiter approached their table. "Did you save room for dessert?"

"I think we're finished," Charese said coolly.

They drove home in complete silence and entered their house. Scott turned on the lights on the Christmas tree and sank down on the sofa. Charese took a seat opposite him.

Scott wrung his hands. "Charese, this is a long, complicated story that I should have told you when we first started dating."

"Go on."

"Well, to begin with, my name isn't Craig Spillman."

"That's what I thought." Her voice was as cold as ice. "So who are you?"

"Scott Simms," he blurted out.

"Okay. So let's hear the rest of the story."

Scott began with the fights he'd had with his father and his flight from Utah. It took over an hour, but eventually he'd told the whole story, with the exception of his marriage to Teresa.

Charese sat shaking her head. "So our whole life together is nothing more than a fraud."

"Sweetheart, I never meant to hurt you."

"Well, you didn't succeed." She stood up and turned away from Scott. The only lights in the room were those on the tree, and they cast their kaleidoscope of colors over Charese as she stood weeping.

"How could you do this to me?" She spun on her heel, marched down the hall, and slammed the bedroom door.

Scott was miserable as he sat on the sofa. *The only two women I've loved and I've screwed things up royally with both of them. Can't I do anything right?*

CHAPTER 44

Thursday, December 24, 2009

The less you say the better," Charese said bitterly. "I've found a place to live over in Hamilton and Dr. Strope has agreed to hire me. I've been moving my things out of your house over the past few days."

"Charese, please, please forgive me. I don't want things to end this way."

"Well Craig, or Scott, or whatever your name is, you should have thought of that several years ago before you started lying to me." She stalked out of the house with a load of clothing draped over her arm. "I'll be back to get the rest of my things next week. When I'm through, I'll leave my key on the table."

"Charese, I'm begging you. Please reconsider." Scott hung his head as he pleaded with her.

She hooked the door with her foot and pulled it shut behind her. A moment later, Scott heard her car door slam. He sank down on the sofa and buried his face in his hands. He'd never felt so rejected and dejected in his life. A moment later, the front door opened and Charese marched back into the house. He looked up expectantly, but she hurried back down the hallway without even glancing in his direction. A few minutes later, she reappeared with another batch of clothing.

"I talked to a lawyer over in Hamilton this morning. He's not sure if I even need to file for divorce since the man I supposedly married is dead." She flung the door open and marched out to her car. When she reappeared, Scott forced himself to his feet.

"Charese, please listen to me." He stepped toward her.

"Touch me and you'll regret it," she snarled.

"Isn't there anyway you'd reconsider?" he begged.

She shook her head violently. "Not a chance." She started back down the hall; then stopped, and with her jaw set firmly said, "And who is this Teresa, anyway?"

Scott recoiled as if he'd been struck with a board. "Teresa?"

"Oh, don't pretend you don't know who she is. I found out all about her. The Internet is a wonderful thing."

After taking the last of her clothing to her car, Charese tramped back into the front room. "Craig, I have one request. Please don't come looking for me."

"I . . . I," he held his hand out toward her. "Please, Charese."

She shook her head. "Have a merry Christmas, you . . . you liar!"

Scott sank back down on the couch as Charese slammed the door behind her. He felt as if his very soul had been ripped from his body. The gray Christmas dawn found him still sitting on the couch with nothing to look forward to. He forced himself to kneel down by the Christmas tree and pick up the gift he'd bought for Charese. He opened the box and removed the bracelet. A silver band had three small diamonds set on each end and the words *Charese and Craig forever* were inscribed. He returned to the couch and read the words over and over again. Finally, it dropped from his hand as he fell into a troubled sleep.

CHAPTER 45

Thursday, July 4, 2013

Scott sat in the Walmart snow cone booth at Rand Park. It was finally dark enough for the fireworks to begin. Since Bill Lowder had been transferred to Omaha, Scott has been promoted to general manager of the Keokuk store. He found the work rewarding, and he often put in much longer hours than expected. Since Charese had left, he'd immersed himself in work. Amazingly, he'd only seen her twice since they'd parted ways more than three years before. Once when he'd been served with divorce papers—he guessed Charese wanted to make sure—and he'd seen her in the courtroom. She ignored him completely. The second time was when he bumped into her at the Halloween pumpkin walk in Nauvoo. When she'd seen him, she'd turned and walked away without saying a word.

Scott had volunteered to man the Fourth of July booth so that all his employees who had families could celebrate the holiday. He couldn't count the number of snow cones he'd made during the holiday celebration. The first firework shot into the sky and exploded into a shower of silver-white sparks that rained down on the Mississippi.

Taking the cue, the lights on the Ferris wheel clicked off along with those on the merry-go-round and the tilt-a-whirl. Scott switched off the string of lights that hung around the snow cone booth. Within a few seconds, all of the lights had been extinguished, throwing the park into darkness. For the next twenty minutes, fireworks whistled, exploded, and sent flashes of color over the enraptured crowd.

The crowd erupted in applause as the fireworks show ended. Scott turned the lights back on and began cleaning the snow cone machine. He backed his truck to the side of the booth and grabbed onto the ice shaver to move it to the bed of the truck.

"Can I give you a hand with that?" a voice said out of the darkness.

"I'd appreciate it," Scott said. "It's pretty heavy."

A heavyset man with a military haircut stepped out of the shadows, grabbed one end of the machine, and helped load it into the truck.

"Thanks," Scott said with a nod of his head.

"No problem—Scott."

Scott started to correct the man, but he saw the man wink his eye as he turned to leave. "Wait. Who are you? Do I know you?"

The man stopped, turned, and stepped back into the square of light. "My name's Rob Norton." He extended his hand and Scott shook it. "I was married to Charese, before you were."

"Oh," Scott said meekly.

"Don't worry. I'm not going to blow your cover. I was just passing through and I bumped into Charese over in Galesburg."

Scott looked puzzled. "I thought she was in Hamilton."

Rob shrugged his shoulders,. "I don't know about that. She was having lunch at the Rib Shack when I pulled in for lunch. Anyway, to make a long story short, we had lunch together. I hadn't talked to her since we got divorced so you two could get married. I asked her how that was going and she filled me in on your situation. I guess she's still pretty steamed about the whole thing." Rob patted Scott on the shoulder. "I don't understand all of it, but enough, I guess. Anyway, I decided I might as well come through Keokuk and drop by Walmart to see what you looked like—just curious, I guess. They told me you were down here running the snow cone machine, so I've been watching you for a little while. You seem like an okay guy."

Scott looked around to see if anyone was listening to the conversation, but everyone was busy cleaning up after the event. He wondered what Rob wanted. "Are you still in the military?" he finally blurted out.

"Just retired, so I thought I'd tour the good old US of A before I settle down somewhere."

"Oh."

Rob reached out and grabbed Scott's shoulder. "Take care." He turned on his heel and walked into the darkness. Scott sank down on one of the folding chairs in the booth.

What a mess I've made of my life.

CHAPTER 46

WEDNESDAY, DECEMBER 16, 2015

Scott entered his office at ten o'clock in the morning and found a stack of mail on the corner of his desk. Beneath the envelopes was his weekly edition of the *Davis County Clipper*. In the years he'd been subscribing, he was amazed at how much his hometown had changed and how much it remained the same. He unfolded the *Clipper* and read the front page. "I guess Bountiful has grown up," he muttered as he read the articles. He thumbed through the paper and suddenly he felt as if his heart stopped. There was an obituary for Randall Simms. It was very brief. Scott read it carefully.

> *Randall Simms, husband, father, and grandfather, passed away Monday, December 14, from causes incident to age. He was born June 12, 1937, in Salt Lake City, Utah. He married Colleen Masters, August 3, 1962; they were later sealed in the Salt Lake Temple, February 15, 1985. Funeral services will be held at 11 a.m., Saturday, December 19, at the LDS chapel at 2505 South Davis Blvd. in Bountiful. A viewing will be held Friday night from 6 to 8 p.m. and from 9:45 a.m. until 10:45 a.m. at the church prior to the services.*

There was no picture accompanying the obituary. Scott looked at the clock over his desk—10:45. Quickly, he brought up Google Maps on his computer. Bountiful, Utah, was eighteen hours and twenty-five minutes from Keokuk. *I can't believe it. He's dead.* Scott felt as if a weight had just been lifted off his shoulders. He sank back in his chair. *What will happen to Mom?* I ought to be there—not for him, but for her. *If I leave now, I can make it to Bountiful in time for the viewing.* He stepped out into the bustling store and saw one of his assistant managers, Ben Spires, over in the men's clothing department.

"Ben," Scott called out and waved his hand. Ben walked over to his boss.

"You need something?"

"I've had a family emergency come up. I've got to leave immediately. I hate to drop this all in your lap, so close to Christmas, but I've got to go."

"No problem. What happened?"

"A death in the family." Scott stepped back into his office and grabbed his jacket. "I'm not sure when I'll be back."

"I understand. Take your time. We'll be okay."

Scott jumped in his truck and sped to his house where he grabbed a few items of clothing. Fifteen minutes later, he pulled into the Hy-Vee gas station on Main Street, filled up, and started the long drive back home. He knew he couldn't drive it all in one stretch, but he figured he'd get as far as he could, find a place to sleep, and carry on the next day. His emotions swung back and forth between relief and guilt.

By the time he reached North Platte, Nebraska, it was nearly ten o'clock at night. He had stopped twice for gas and dinner and now he was fighting to keep his eyes open. He shook his head to clear the cobwebs and rolled down his window. The cold air shocked him for a minute but he knew he needed to stop for the night. An exit sign on I-80 advertised a Holiday Inn Express, and a few minutes later, Scott pulled into the parking lot and paid for a room. Snow was beginning to fall as he dropped off to sleep as soon as his head hit the pillow.

He awoke the next morning, grabbed breakfast, and headed toward his destination. The snow had stopped and I-80 had been plowed. "Ten more hours," he murmured, "If the weather holds."

PART THREE

Metamorphosis

CHAPTER 47

Tuesday, June 14, 1983

"Colleen he'll be back!" Randall Simms pushed the chair back from the dining table. "Once he gets hungry enough, he'll be back."

Colleen wiped her eyes with her handkerchief. "He's been gone since Saturday. Where would he go?"

"He's a big boy. Let him blow off some steam and he'll come back with his tail between his legs." With that, Randall marched out the kitchen door into the back yard. It was a beautiful late spring night. Crickets were chirping and the sun had just sunk behind the hills on Antelope Island. He walked across the lawn to the small shade shelter he and Scott had built two summers before and slumped down into one of the Adirondack chairs that were arranged in a semicircle around a fire pit. *Where are you?* he thought. *Why can't you ever do what you're told to do?* He held his head in his hands as he tried to think where his son might be. He'd already called all of Scott's friends to see if he might be hanging out with one of them, but with no success. He felt embarrassed to walk through the neighborhood and ask if anyone had seen his son, but finally he'd swallowed his pride and done just that. Milton Carlisle thought he'd seen Scott walking down Orchard Drive, but he couldn't remember whether that was Friday or Saturday. No one else had noticed him.

Colleen had fallen apart. When Scott didn't come home Sunday, she'd been beside herself. Apparently, she'd talked to the bishop after church because he'd called Randall and asked him to meet with him on Sunday. As embarrassing as that was going to be, he guessed it would calm Colleen's fears. Randall was sure his son would return by Monday, but that hadn't happened, and now they were ending the fourth day since he'd left.

Randall was beside himself with worry and angry beyond belief at his son for doing such a stupid thing and putting his mother through such agony. He rocked back and forth in the chair trying to clear his mind. Night fell completely and the crickets were joined by the buzz of mosquitoes. Randall looked at the lighted windows of their home and willed his son to return.

The back door opened and their daughter, Jill, stepped onto the porch. "Dad, are you out here?"

"Back here under the shelter."

She skipped down the steps and crossed the lawn. "Dad, where's Scotty?"

He swung his head back and forth. "I don't know. I can't believe he's stupid enough to stay away this long."

"Dad, he's not stupid," she said in defense of her brother.

"Well, this is a pretty stupid thing to do."

Jill sat down on the edge of one of the other chairs. "What are you going to do about it?"

"Me? Wait for him to come to his senses," he said with a sniff.

"What if he's hurt? What if he's lying somewhere bleeding?"

A chill ran down Randall's spine; the thought that his son might be injured had never entered his mind. "Jill, he's a big boy. He knows how to take care of himself." He pushed himself to his feet and his daughter followed. He started to feel a little guilty. "Jill, if he doesn't come home by tomorrow, I'll try to find someone who can look for him."

"Like a private detective?"

"I suppose."

"What about the cops?"

"Your mother has already reported him as a missing person to the police. But he's eighteen and we have to recognize that." They reached the steps to the back porch.

Jill looked into her father's eyes. "Dad, what happened? How come Scotty ran away?"

Randall stiffened. "He was just being unreasonable. We disagreed on something."

Jill shook her head and entered the house. Randall looked up at the stars overhead. *Come home.*

CHAPTER 48

Sunday, June 19, 1983

Randall sat in the foyer of the church waiting for Bishop Gerber to finish an interview. He tapped his fingers nervously on the arm of the chair. *Colleen must have told him about Scotty. Why else would he ask me to come to his office?*

The door opened and a young couple Randall barely recognized stepped out into the hallway. Bishop Gerber shook each of their hands and then spotted Randall sitting across the foyer. He stepped over to Randall and extended his hand. "Brother Simms, thank you for coming here on such short notice."

Randall nodded his head, took the bishop's hand, and was pulled to his feet. A moment later, they'd crossed the foyer and entered the bishop's office.

"Have a seat," Bishop Gerber said as he sat down behind his desk. Randall sat down a little warily. "Sister Simms decided not to come with you?"

"She's tied up at the moment," Randall said. In fact, he hadn't even told her about the phone call from the bishop. He steeled himself for the questions about Scott from Bishop Gerber.

"Well, this is pretty short notice, but I'm wondering if you'd serve on the Fourth of July breakfast committee? It's the elders quorum's turn to be in charge and you're such a good organizer, I thought you'd be a great asset to them."

Randall was stunned. This had nothing do about Scotty's disappearance. "Sure, I guess," he managed to say. "When are they meeting?"

"Tuesday night. President Beal will be contacting you." He rose from behind his desk and took Randall's hand in his. "I appreciate this, Brother Simms." He reached for the door handle. "How's your family?"

Randall took a deep breath, "They're just fine. We all have our problems, but all in all we're just fine"

"I'm so happy Scott earned that scholarship to BYU. I hope he's still planning on a mission."

"Yeah, I think so." Randall hurried out of the building to his car. *Obviously he doesn't know Scotty's run away. Well, I'm sure he'll be home before long.* He drove slowly homeward wondering why the bishop had asked him to serve on this committee. He hadn't been attending church very regularly. He barely knew Clarence Beal, the elders quorum president. *He's just trying to give me a no-nothing job in hopes he can reactivate me.* Randall slammed his hand down on the steering wheel. *Well, he can just take that job and . . .* Suddenly, a thought raced through his mind and a broad smile spread over his face. *We'll make this a breakfast they'll never forget.*

CHAPTER 49

Tuesday, June 21, 1983

Clarence Beal, the elders quorum president, shook everyone's hand as they entered the Relief Society room. "Thanks for coming to this first meeting of the Fourth of July breakfast committee. I guess it's the elders turn to be in charge." He stood behind the table at the front of the room. "Brother Carlisle, would you mind opening with prayer?"

"My pleasure," he stood and offered a short prayer.

"Thank you, I appreciate all of you coming. I think if we divide up the food we can make this happen without a lot of trouble for anyone."

Randall cleared his throat. "Brother Beal, I've been thinking about the breakfast."

"I think we all have, Brother Simms."

Randall rubbed his chin. "You know we always seem to have the same menu—scrambled eggs, bacon, and pancakes."

The other six people on the committee nodded their heads. Brother Beal, said, "Well, I think that's what everybody expects. That's what we've done every year that I've lived in the ward."

"I suppose, but I've been thinking we might change it up a little this year. What if we had ham, omelets, muffins, and fresh fruit? We could make it a little classier."

"Why?" asked Sister Rawlings. "Everybody seems to like what we've had before."

Randall's jaw clenched. "It's just a thought."

"Could we really keep up with that many omelets? I mean, we usually get nearly three hundred people out to the breakfast." Brother Mohn, the high priest group leader, scratched his chin. He looked at Randall who had a scowl on his face. "Not that it's a bad idea."

"All it takes is a little planning. We could beat the eggs ahead of time so they could be poured on the griddles out of pitchers. They we'd add the bacon bits or ham or whatever. They wouldn't take any longer to cook than the usual scrambled eggs and they'd be a heck of a lot better tasting," Randall said trying to keep his voice even.

"I don't know," Sister Rawlings countered. "I've made omelets for my family and it takes a lot longer than just scrambling eggs. It uses more eggs too."

Randall thrust out his jaw. "Maybe you just need to get organized."

Brother Mohn tried to head off a direct confrontation. "Would you make muffins or get store-bought?"

"I don't suppose it matters if we're going to go back to the same old menu," Randall said coldly.

"Well, suppose we do go the omelet route, who would you have make the muffins?"

"Well," Randall smiled and stood up, "I've already talked to Dick's bakery and they can supply them at a really good price."

"Wait a minute," Sister Rawlings interjected, "You've already talked to the bakery? I hope you didn't order the muffins."

Randall bristled. "Of course I did. I nailed down the price and went ahead and ordered thirty dozen."

"Without asking the rest of the committee? This is the first time we've met."

"Well, it seems like we're dragging our feet. The breakfast isn't that far away. Somebody has to make a decision; am I right? I thought I'd save everyone else some time and energy."

It was as if a blanket had descended over the group.

"Okay, fine. I'll cancel the order," Randall said, sitting back down.

Brother Mohn raised his hands in front of him. "Brother Simms, let's just see what decisions we can make before you run off and cancel the order . . ."

Randall glared at Sister Rawlings.

"You know, maybe Brother Simms is right. We might need a couple of more grills, but that can be arranged; and if we're not doing pancakes, we might have enough already." Brother Mohn nodded his head. "What's our budget, Brother Beal?"

"Same as last year, a dollar per person."

"How much are the muffins, Brother Simms?"

Randall cleared his throat, "Ninety-two dollars plus tax."

"Should be tax free," Brother Beal said.

"So can we do fresh fruit and omelets for about two hundred dollars?"

Sister Rawlings shook her head. "I don't think so. Fruit is so expensive."

"Of course we can," Randall said pointedly. "It just takes some planning and someone willing to go negotiate."

Brother Mohn smiled. "Brother Simms, it seems like you're pretty good at this, why don't you go price out all of the food necessary for the breakfast you'd like to prepare and tell us what you find out at our next meeting. If you can bring it in under three hundred dollars, I say let's go ahead."

"Okay." Randall smiled and settled back in his chair.

Brother Beal stood back up. "Well, unless there's something else, let's have a closing prayer. Sister Rawlings, would you mind?"

"When are we going to meet again? The fourth is only a couple of weeks away," she asked as she rose to her feet.

"Next Sunday. Same time, same place," Brother Beal said.

"Good luck," she said, shaking her head and staring at Randall before she closed their meeting.

The next Sunday, Randall reported that they could get all of the food for less than three hundred dollars. The rest of them agreed to his menu.

When he went to pick up the muffins, he paid for them out of his own pocket. The rest of the food cost just over three hundred dollars. Except for people having to wait while the omelets cooked, the breakfast was a success.

CHAPTER 50

Friday, July 8, 1983

Randall and Colleen sat silently in the storefront office of Gus Anderson's. The portly balding man sat on the other side of his desk.

"He apparently purchased a bus ticket to San Jose, California."

Colleen wiped her eyes with a tissue. "And what did he do after he arrived in San Jose, Mr. Anderson?"

"Well, that's where it gets interesting. As far as we can tell, he hasn't applied for work in San Jose."

Randall stood up. "So, what you're saying is that we really don't know where he is. Is that right?"

Gus nodded his head. "I've put a lot of hours in trying to find your son, but he seems to have found a way to vanish."

Colleen shook her head. "What do we do next?"

"I could keep taking your money," Anderson said, "But really, until he does something to call attention to himself, there's not a lot we can do. The local police have put out a missing person report on him, but that hasn't turned up anything either. I've contacted the San Jose PD and they're looking for him too."

Colleen tugged on Randall's hand. "Let's drive to San Jose and look for him."

Gus Anderson stood up from behind his desk. "You can certainly do that, but I would point out that San Jose is a big city—the third biggest in California. The chance of running into your son is pretty remote."

"So what do we do?" she cried in desperation.

"As hard as this might sound, I think you just have to wait for him to decide he wants to come home." Anderson walked around his desk and led them to the door. "If I hear anything, I'll let you know."

Randall and Colleen walked into the parking lot. Randall climbed into the car and started the engine. "You heard what he said. We just need to wait until Scott decides to come home."

"And how long do we wait?"

Randall backed out of the parking place. "Well, BYU starts next month. I can't believe he'd be dumb enough to pass up his scholarship."

"Randall, he's not dumb." A thought entered her mind and a smile crossed Colleen's face. "So even if he doesn't come home, we can go find him on campus."

Randall nodded his head. "I'll call the registrar's office tomorrow and see if they've heard anything from Scotty."

They drove home in complete silence. Jill was waiting when they walked through the door. "Any word?" she asked expectantly.

"Apparently he took the bus to San Jose," Randall said.

"What's in San Jose?"

"I don't know."

CHAPTER 51

"This isn't like any ward dinner I ever remember," Randall said as he helped spread a blanket on the floor of the cultural hall. After the Fourth of July breakfast, he had only been in the church twice since Scott's disappearance. His call to the registrar's office at BYU had been frustrating. According to the woman he'd talked to, Scott had made no effort to enroll at the university.

Colleen nodded her head. "They said this was going to be a special night."

Jill sat down on the blanket and looked around the room. It was crowded with each family sitting on a blanket. The folding doors to the overflow were shut and everyone was crammed onto the basketball court. Even the curtain to the stage was shut.

Bishop Gerber stood in front of the stage and tapped the microphone with his hand; it popped several times. "Brothers and sisters, welcome to a night in Bethlehem. We've asked Brother Frank Porter to offer an opening prayer and a blessing on the food. Once he has finished, would each family send one member out into the hallway by the kitchen? They will bring back a special gift to you. When everyone has their gift, I'll give you some more instructions. Brother Porter." He handed the microphone to the tall, lanky man who stood in front of the stage.

Once the invocation and blessing were offered, Randall pointed his finger at his daughter and motioned for her to go. Jill stood up and followed the crowd toward the kitchen. When it was her turn, she was handed a small two-inches high burlap bag. It was heavier than she expected, but as she started to untie the strings that held it shut, she was told to wait until further instructions were given before opening it. She returned to her family.

"What were you given?" her mother asked.

"This," Jill replied as she handed the small bag to her mother.

"Brothers and sisters," Bishop Gerber said. "If you'll open your bag, you'll find what you need to purchase your dinner." Colleen untied the string and dumped out a dozen small coins. Each one was stamped with the words *widow's mite*.

At that moment, the doors to the overflow were pushed open revealing six canvas shade shelters that had been set up behind the folding doors. Tables had been set up inside the shelters forming a solid line across the opening. Signs hung from the shelters telling what kind of food was available.

The Simms family joined the rest of the congregation as they made their way down the line and filled their plates with food. Randall tried to pay with the widow's mites, but they were returned as a remembrance of the evening. Then they returned to their blanket, sat down, and ate their dinner.

Randall shook his head. "It would be a lot more comfortable eating at a table." Colleen smiled and nodded her head.

"It tastes great," Jill said as she spread some chopped chicken on a piece of flatbread, folded it, and took a bite.

They had almost finished eating when suddenly Craig Foster walked through one door of the cultural hall. He was the six-foot-seven-inch center on the high school basketball team. Dressed in a flowing white robe, he walked through the crowd until he reached a small platform that had been set up in one corner of the room. He stepped onto the platform, turned, and looked down on the crowd. A spotlight illuminated his face. The room became instantly quiet.

Randall felt goose bumps rise on his arms.

"Hail, Mary, thou art highly favored, the Lord is with thee: blessed art thou among women."

Brother and Sister Cluff were sitting in front of Craig beneath the basketball standard. She was dressed in a flowing robe and had a scarf over her head. As Brother Foster spoke, she stood up and put her hands over her eyes.

"Fear not, Mary, for thou hast found favor with God. And, behold, thou shalt conceive in thy womb, and bring forth a son, and shall call his name, Jesus. He shall be great, and shall be called the Son of the Highest: and the Lord God shall give unto him the throne of his father David."

Sister Cluff extended her hands toward Brother Foster. "How shall this be?"

"The Holy Ghost shall come upon thee, and the power of the Highest shall overshadow thee: therefore also that holy thing which shall be born of thee shall be called the Son of God."

Sister Cluff sank to her knees.

Randall felt a swell of emotion in his breast. *What would it be like to be visited by an angel?*

"And, behold, thy cousin Elisabeth, she hath also conceived a son in her old age: and this is the sixth month with her, who was called barren. For with God nothing shall be impossible." He pointed across the room to the far side of the cultural hall.

Sister Cluff stood up again. "Behold the handmaid of the Lord; be it unto me according to thy word."

She's following the command without even questioning. Imagine the turmoil she must have felt. Randall felt tears forming.

Brother Foster stepped down from the platform and left the room. Sister Cluff began making her way through the crowd that covered the floor of the cultural hall. When she reached the far end, Sister Powell, who was seven months pregnant, was helped to her feet and a chair provided for her. Sister Cluff made it to her side and sank to her knees again.

"Hail, Elizabeth."

Sister Powell suddenly straightened and placed her hands on her ample belly. "Blessed art thou among women, and blessed is the fruit of thy womb. And whence is this to me, that the mother of my Lord should come to me? For, lo, as soon as the voice of thy salutation sounded in mine ears, the babe leaped in my womb for joy."

Sister Cluff stood up and said, "My soul doth magnify the Lord, and my spirit hath rejoiced in God my Saviour. For he hath regarded the low estate of his handmaiden: for, behold from henceforth all generations shall call me blessed."

Slowly, Sister Powell rose from her chair and made her way out of the room. Sister Cluff made her way back across the room to the side of her husband, who was playing the role of Joseph. Randall studied her face as she passed by. She looked frightened. Brother Cluff watched her come and began to shake his head. Sister Cluff saw the frown on his face, stopped, and sat down on a blanket some distance from her husband. He turned his face away from her.

Don't you understand? Randall wanted to ask Joseph. Although this was an old story, it took on new meaning as it was acted out.

But at that moment, Brother Foster slipped back into the room, although he was hardly invisible being clothed in white and standing as tall as he did. He made his way to Brother Cluff and said, "Joseph, thou son of David, fear not to take unto thee Mary thy wife: for that which is conceived in her is of the Holy Ghost. And she shall bring forth a son, and thou shall call his name, Jesus: for he shall save his people from their sins."

It was as if Randall had never really understood the story of the birth of the Savior. An unbidden feeling of warmth began to spread through his body and he felt tears running down his cheeks. A desire to live a better life sprang into his heart. He began to examine his own behavior and he thought, *He's the Savior about to be born. Can he save me?*

As Brother Foster exited for a second time, Brother Cluff put out his hand toward his wife; she stood up, and joined him. Together, they made their way across the floor toward the overflow. As they approached, the doors were pulled shut across each of the shade shelters, and with their heads bowed they moved back and forth across the cultural hall. The stage curtains opened revealing a manger and a stable complete with cardboard cutouts of animals. Brother and Sister Cluff climbed the steps to the stage and knelt at the side of the manger. Their three-month-old son had been placed in the manger and suddenly he thrust a hand upward and wiggled his fingers to the delight of the congregation.

Brother Foster appeared through doors on the opposite side of the room and four young men dressed in shepherds' garb stood in front of him. "Fear not: for, behold, I bring you good tidings of great joy, which shall be to all people. For unto you is born this day in the city of David a Saviour, which is Christ the Lord. And this shall be a sign unto you; ye shall find the babe wrapped in swaddling clothes, lying in a manger."

Randall's lips formed the words that were being spoken as he retrieved a memory from years past.

Hidden behind the back stage curtains, a dozen members of the ward choir began singing, "Glory to God in the highest and on earth peace, good will toward men."

The shepherds made their way to the stage and knelt down by the manger. The congregation was so still it seemed as if no one was even breathing.

Emotions Randall had kept hidden for decades bubbled to the surface.

One of the shepherds, ten-year-old Stan Morrison, had been blessed with a beautiful, clear singing voice. He stood up, stepped behind the manger so he faced the audience, and in the sweetest voice imaginable began to sing, "I am a Child of God." Chills ran down Randall's spine. As the young boy finished, he looked into the congregation and it seemed as if his eyes bored into Randall's. "And so are you," he said with conviction.

The back door of the cultural hall opened and the bishopric entered dressed as the magi. Bishop Gerber said loudly, "Where is he that is born King of the Jews? For we have seen his star in the east, and are come to worship him."

A thin cable had been stretched from above the overflow doors to the proscenium and a lighted star hung on it. As the wise men pointed at it, the star began to move across the room toward the stage. The bishopric followed the star and when they joined the rest of the people on the stage, they presented their gifts of gold, frankincense, and myrrh. Everyone knelt near the manger. The stage curtain closed.

From behind the curtain Bishop Gerber announced, "Brothers and sisters, thank you for joining us on this special night in Bethlehem. Sister Carol McKay will offer a benediction."

After the closing prayer, Randall helped Colleen with her coat. He bounced the small bag of coins in his hand as they walked to the car. "That was something else," he said softly.

"Yes, it was," Colleen replied as she patted his knee.

"I've never felt the Spirit like that," Jill said from the back seat.

Colleen watched the tears streaming down her husband's face. She reached over and gave him a hug.

CHAPTER 52

Sunday, December 11, 1983

Randall looked in the mirror as he knotted his tie. "Ready?" he called out.

His wife stuck her head into the bedroom. "You're going with us?" she said surprised.

"Of course. Why wouldn't I?"

"I don't know, you just haven't been going to church very often."

Randall shrugged his shoulders. "Well, I'm going today." He walked quickly into the garage. "Don't make us late."

Colleen and Jill scurried after him. "How come you're coming to church, Dad?" Jill asked.

"I felt like it," he said as he backed out of the garage. He checked his watch; it was ten minutes to nine.

When the block of meetings ended, Randall waited for Bishop Gerber outside his office. He arrived, stuck out his hand, and shook Randall's. "How are you, Brother Simms? It's good to see you."

"Fine." He paused for a moment. "Can I get an appointment to meet with you?"

"Of course, is it an emergency?"

Randall shook his head. "No, no, I just need a few minutes of your time."

The bishop unlocked the door to his office and led Randall inside. "Let me look at what Brother Carlisle has set up for me today." He picked up a sheet of paper. "Hmm, looks like I'm free after three o'clock. Does that work for you?"

"I'll be here," Randall answered curtly. He weaved his way through the cluster of people milling around in the foyer, found his wife and daughter, and drove home.

Colleen had left a roast simmering in a crock-pot and it took only a few minutes until they were eating dinner. When they finished, Jill began clearing the table. "I love Christmas," she said cheerfully. "I love the music and everybody seems a little kinder."

"My favorite time of year," her mother replied.

Randall remained quiet. He pushed himself away from the table and walked into the front room where he sat down and started to read the newspaper. "I have an appointment with the bishop at three o'clock," he said.

Colleen was in the kitchen washing the dishes. "What?"

"I said, I have a meeting with the bishop."

"What for?" She was genuinely confused.

"Because I asked for one."

From the tone of his voice it was clear he didn't want to continue with any further explanation. Ten minutes before three Randall said, "I'll be back." He backed the car out of the garage and drove to the church. Bishop Gerber was waiting for him.

"Brother Simms, what can I do for you?" The bishop closed the door and beckoned for Randall to take a seat.

"I wanted to thank you for last night's event."

"You're welcome, although there were a lot of other people who deserve the praise more than I."

Randall nodded his head slightly. "It got me to thinking." He paused and Bishop Gerber waited for him to continue. "Bishop, do you really think you and I are children of God?"

Bishop Gerber smiled broadly. "Of course. Don't you?"

"I don't know. I've never thought much about it."

"Brother Simms, not only are you a child of God, you are one of his chosen ones."

A puzzled look came over Randall's face. "What makes you think that?"

"Because you are. You've been born at a time when the fullness of the gospel is on the earth. You've been baptized and confirmed a member of the Church of Jesus Christ. You are one of a very elect and select few."

Randall looked down at the carpet in front of him. "Bishop, I came from a family who wasn't active in the church at all. I was baptized because all my friends were getting baptized. I didn't serve a mission. I haven't been much of a regular attender." He looked very uncomfortable.

"Brother Simms, only you can change that. This is a church of moral agency. No one can make you do anything you don't want to do."

Randall shook his head. "Maybe it would be easier if you could force me to attend."

Bishop Gerber smiled. "I think that's what a third of the host of heaven thought." He put his elbows on his desk and rested his chin on his hands. "If I might ask, what has brought this about?"

Randall thought about getting up and leaving. This was getting more and more uncomfortable. The bishop waited. Finally Randall settled back in his seat and said, "The little boy who sang last night."

"Stan Morrison. Isn't he talented? He has quite a voice for a ten-year-old."

Randall took a deep breath and exhaled. "It seemed like he was singing directly to me."

"Maybe he was," Bishop Gerber said. They sat silently again for nearly a minute; then the bishop asked, "What's really bothering you, Brother Simms?"

Randall licked his lips. "Bishop can I ask you a question?"

"Of course."

"Let me begin by saying that the Fourth of July committee was really frustrating." Bishop Gerber nodded his head. "Sister Rawlings just seemed like she wanted to dig her heels in and refuse any suggestions I made."

"I've heard rumors," the bishop said with a slight smile.

"Bishop, I've spent my life telling people what they needed to do. It's been part of my job as an engineer. But in the church all I run up against is resistance."

The bishop frowned. "Is that what's bothering you, Brother Simms? That not everybody thinks the way you do?"

"Well, no. I mean, I just seem to upset everybody else at church. That doesn't happen at work. I think it's that everybody feels better than me . . ."

There was a knock on the door. Bishop Gerber stood up, walked to the door, and opened it a crack. His clerk handed him a slip of paper. He glanced at it, nodded his head, and closed the door. Instead of returning to his desk, he seated himself in the chair next to Randall.

"Do you want me to be perfectly frank, Brother Simms?"

"Of course."

"You're not always right."

It was as if someone had slapped him in the face. "What?"

"None of us is always right. We think we're right. Then we get more information and find we were in error." The bishop put his hand on Randall's shoulder. "There's no shame in admitting we were mistaken."

"But you don't work with the people I work with," Randall sputtered.

"No, but I work with some just like them. And you know what? They make mistakes, but so do I. Thankfully we can be forgiven. And honestly, I don't think they like being ordered around by you anymore than you'd like being ordered around yourself."

Randall turned his chair so that he was staring into the bishop's face. He thrust his chin out. "Bishop, I understand what you're saying. I'm sure we all make mistakes, but let me ask you, what do you think I need to be forgiven for?"

Bishop Gerber smiled. "I don't know, Randall. You tell me."

That caught Randall by surprise. "I don't know, really . . ." he waved his hands in front of him.

"Then, if there's nothing to be forgiven for, maybe you don't need the Atonement."

Randall sank back down in his chair and they sat quietly enough they could hear the clock on the wall ticking each second. Finally, with a sigh he said, "Bishop, do you think I'm a negative person? I want an honest answer."

Without missing a beat he replied. "Honestly? Yes."

Randall looked surprised that the bishop had answered so directly. "So, how do I change?"

Bishop Gerber rose to his feet and extended his hands to Randall. "By admitting there's a problem and then solving it." He pulled him to his feet.

"How?"

"Why don't you think about that for a while? You need to come up with your own solution, not one that I've suggested. Why don't you ponder it and see what happens. We can meet again next Sunday and you can tell me what you've decided." He led Randall to the door, opened it, and ushered him into the hallway. "Thanks for the conversation. See you next week."

CHAPTER 53

Sunday, December 18, 1983

Well, Brother Simms, how did your week go?" Bishop Gerber invited him into his office and indicated a seat.

"It has been a pretty miserable week, truthfully. You gave me a lot to think about."

The bishop smiled. "Change, even change for the better, can be miserable."

Randall nodded his head. "Every time I started to say something to one of my employees I'd hear you telling me not to be so judgmental. I can't count how many times that happened."

"It sounds as if you've been doing some introspection. Have you reached any conclusion?"

Randall looked miserable. "Bishop, I've come up with something I think might work. I thought I'd run it by you."

"Okay."

He looked uncomfortable as he continued, "I have an empty one of those five-gallon water bottles that go on the cooler at work." He looked at the bishop to make sure he understood.

"Go on."

"I thought I'd asked my wife to help me and have her tell me when I did or said something negative, and every time she does that I'll put a quarter in the bottle."

The bishop rubbed his chin. "That worries me a little; I think you might already have some stress in your marriage, and this might increase it."

Randall nodded his head. "You're right, I think I've already put stress on our marriage."

The bishop smiled. "So who gets the quarters?"

"Oh? Colleen does. I can't believe there will be many of them. I'm pretty sure I can change once I put my mind to it."

Bishop Gerber tried to keep a straight face. "Don't be too sure, Brother Simms. Habits are very hard to break."

"Well, this isn't like smoking, I'm not addicted. I think you just have to make up your mind and change."

The bishop smiled. "Well, it sounds like a plan. Good luck. By the way, what happens when your wife isn't around? Like work?"

"She'll just have to trust me."

"You seem relieved."

"Bishop, I did what you said. I pondered the problem and this is the solution I came up with."

"Let me know how it goes."

Randall drove home with resolve in his heart. Once he was in the garage, he retrieved the empty water bottle he'd brought home from work and carried it into the kitchen. "Colleen, where are you?"

"In here," she replied from the living room.

"I need to talk to you." He took the bottle into the living room, sat down in his recliner, and put the bottle on the floor next to it.

"What's that for?" she asked.

It took a few minutes for him to explain the purpose for the bottle. When he finished he asked, "So, will you do that for me?"

Colleen smoothed her skirt with her hands. "Are you sure, Randall?"

He nodded his head. "What could go wrong? I'll end up putting a couple of quarters in the bottle, and I'll quit being so negative."

"I don't want you getting mad at me," she said softly.

"I won't. Why would you think I couldn't do this?" he barked.

Colleen smiled. "That will be a quarter, please."

Randall sat up straight, shook his head, reached in his pocket and dropped a quarter in the bottle.

Six days later, on Christmas Eve, he was beginning to wonder if this was such a good idea. The bottom of the bottle was covered with coins.

CHAPTER 54

Sunday, December 23, 1984

Randall reached over and took his wife's hand in his. The high school Madrigal choir was singing in sacrament meeting and the music was beautiful and uplifting. He turned his head and looked at the Clifford family who were sitting two rows in front of them and to their left. He and Colleen had picked the Cliffords for a Twelve Days of Christmas project. Tonight, Jill would deliver the tenth day of Christmas gift to them. It had been fun to leave a present on their doorstep each night, ring the bell, and run away before they could discover who was doing the Twelve Days for them.

The choir finished their last number and Bishop Gerber stood behind the pulpit. "Brothers and sisters, we've been treated to a heavenly choir. I hope the rest of your holidays are as beautiful and uplifting as the music we've just heard. Brother Randall Simms will offer the benediction. Merry Christmas."

Randall made his way to the pulpit and offered the closing prayer. When "Amen" was offered, he started to leave the stand when Bishop Gerber reached up and stopped him. "Thank you, Brother Simms."

"Thank you, Bishop. This has been a wonderful year, thanks to you."

The bishop winked at Randall. "You're quite an inspiration to me. I wasn't sure you could pull it off, but you've proven me wrong."

He looked at Colleen and Jill sitting in the audience. "Your family looks much happier too."

Randall bowed his head. "I just wish we knew where Scott was."

"No word?"

Randall shook his head. "I need to find him so I can beg his forgiveness."

"I wish I knew how to help."

The rest of the people on the stand had left and were making their way out of the chapel. Randall patted the bishop on the shoulder and turned to leave.

"Have you made a decision on your sealing date?" the bishop whispered.

"February. We're trying to get Colleen's folks here and that's the soonest they can come. They're quite frail. Probably the fifth."

"Wonderful."

Randall joined his wife and daughter and they walked down the aisle together. They left the church, and ten minutes later they entered the kitchen. The water bottle sat in one corner of the room, more than half full of quarters. He patted it with his hand as he walked past on the way to the bedroom. It had been over two weeks since he'd had to drop a quarter in the jug.

They sat down for dinner and while they were eating Randall asked, "Sweetheart, what are you going to do with your quarters?"

Colleen smiled sweetly. "Oh, I have a plan. But I'd like to keep it secret for the moment."

"I'll bet there's a couple of hundred dollars worth."

She nodded her head. "It's so heavy I can't move it by myself. I think I'll have to . . ." she broke into song, "Tip it over and pour it out."

He laughed. "I can't believe how quickly that filled up, especially at first."

"I was really afraid it was going to make you angry. You've made me so proud of you."

"I couldn't have done it without you." He stood up and tried to wrestle the bottle out of the corner. It was too heavy. "Maybe three hundred dollars."

CHAPTER 55

Thursday, February 14, 1985

Randall parked the car in the garage and climbed the steps to the back porch. He took a deep breath before he opened the kitchen door. He could smell the enticing aroma of cherry pie. *I'm so lucky.*

His wife was sitting at the kitchen table. An open scrapbook was in front of her. She stood up as Randall entered the room, threw her arms around him, and kissed him.

"Wow! What did I do to deserve that?" he said. "Not that I'm complaining."

Colleen smiled. "I'm just so happy we're going to the temple tomorrow to be sealed."

Randall hugged her. "If I hadn't been so dumb, we'd have been there long ago."

"You're not dumb, sweetheart."

"I'm glad I have you fooled." He peered over her shoulder at the scrapbook. "What's that?"

"Oh, I found his scrapbook while I was cleaning out the hall closet."

Randall reached out and turned the open book toward him. Overcome with emotion, he dropped his chin on his chest. "Can you ever forgive me?" he blurted out.

"For what?"

He pointed at a picture of eight-year-old Scott sitting in a swing at the park. "For driving him away." He sank down onto one a chair and absently turned the pages.

"Randall, there's enough blame to go around. What's done is done and you can't change it."

He nodded his head. "But where is he?"

Tears filled Colleen's eyes as well. "I don't know, but somehow I feel he's still alive."

"I wonder what it will take to bring him home."

Colleen put her hand on top of her husband's. "I guess we'll just have to wait and see." She brushed the tears from her cheeks. "But before you get too maudlin, I have a Valentine's Day surprise for you."

Randall straightened in his chair. "What kind of surprise?" He looked expectantly at his wife.

"Stand up and close your eyes."

Randall did as he was told. "Now what?"

She took his arm. "Follow me, but don't open your eyes until I tell you." She led him gently out of the kitchen and into the living room. "Ready? One, two, three."

Randall opened his eyes and his jaw dropped open. In one corner of the living room sat a baby grand piano. "What? How? I mean, we can't afford . . ."

"It's paid for."

"How?"

Colleen pointed to the empty water jug next to the piano. "It isn't new, but there were enough quarters in the bottle to pay for it. I think it will make Jill's day. She's always wanted a piano. Now she won't have to go to the church to practice."

"Well, at least my negativity led to something positive," he chuckled. "I had no idea."

She led him to the couch and sat down. "Are you ready for tomorrow?"

"More than ready."

"Sweetheart, the past is past and tomorrow we start a brand new future together." She kissed him again. "You've made me so happy."

"And you've made me a better man."

CHAPTER 56

Sunday, March 18, 1990

Randall and Colleen sat on the couch outside the stake president's door. "I'll bet they want to call you as Relief Society president."

Colleen shook her head. "I don't think so."

"Well, I don't think they want to call me to anything."

"Why not? You're such a good man."

"I'm glad you think so."

The door opened and President Leonard Cason stepped into the foyer. "Brother and Sister Simms," he shook their hands, "Please come into the office." He led them to two chairs placed in front of his desk. "How are you doing?"

"Just fine, President," Colleen answered.

"How is Jill doing? How are her kids? She has two, doesn't she?"

Colleen beamed. "She and Dan are doing great. Her daughter, Jenny, is just like her mother, and little Jim is the spitting image of his father."

"How old are they now?"

"Jimmy will be four in August and Jenny is becoming a terrible two."

"Time certainly flies." He smiled broadly. "I remember Jill and Dan's reception. Those banana splits you had were unforgettable."

Randall spoke up. "That was a great year. Colleen and I were sealed in February and Jill and Dan were married in the temple in December."

President Cason nodded his head. "Isn't that what this is all about—families being sealed for eternity?"

Randall and Colleen nodded their heads.

President Cason rested his elbows on his desk and interlaced his fingers. "You're probably wondering why I asked you to come down here."

"It has created a little nervousness," Randall chuckled.

"Well, Sister Simms," he began. Randall put his hand on top of his wife's and nodded his head as he smiled at her. "I have a question to ask you."

"Yes, President," she said softly.

"Is there any reason we shouldn't call your husband as elders quorum president?"

"What?" Randall said.

Colleen smiled broadly. "No reason at all. He'll do a great job. He's already responsible for activating half a dozen families in our ward through scouting. We have a whole lot of Eagle Scouts who owe their rank to my husband's persistence."

"I know, Sister Simms. That's one reason we feel he's the right man for the job." He focused on Randall. "So, Brother Simms, will you accept that calling?"

Randall shook his head slightly. "Are you sure, President?"

"Absolutely. We've prayed about it and felt inspired to call you. Randall, I've watched you over the past ten years and quite honestly, I've never seen a more faithful member, nor have I seen one who exemplifies the love of the Savior more than you."

"President, I haven't always been that way."

"Oh? Is there something I should know—some reason I shouldn't extend the call?" His forehead creased.

Colleen patted Randall's hand. "President, my husband is the most humble, patient man I've ever known. He'll be a wonderful quorum president."

President Cason smiled. "I know better than to disagree with your wife. Will you accept the call, Brother Simms?"

"If you think I can do it," Randall said softly.

"Wonderful. We'll make the change next Sunday. I need to know as soon as possible whom you want for counselors so we can get them called. Please pray about it and when you have the names, give me a call." He rose from behind his desk and hugged Randall. "Congratulations." As they were leaving his office, President Cason paused. "You know, Brother Simms, when I was called as stake president a little over a year ago, I had the same reaction you did. Isn't it amazing how we can flash back and think of every reason we're not worthy for the call?" He shook his head, "I've learned that none of us can do the work alone, but with the Lord's help we can achieve miracles. You'll be great."

CHAPTER 57

Tuesday, March 16, 1999

Randall took Colleen's hand as they entered the stake president's office. President Richard Newman, Scott's old friend, was sitting behind his desk talking on the phone. He beckoned to them with his free hand and indicated the chairs in front of his desk. "That will be fine, Brother Callister. I'll see you then. Goodbye." He hung up the phone. He stood up as did his two counselors who were seated on either side of him. "Brother and Sister Simms, thank you for coming. Please, have a seat." He reached over his desk and shook their hands. "How are the two of you doing?"

"Just great," Randall said.

"How's the family?"

"Jill and Dan moved to Cedar City just after Christmas. We haven't seen enough of them and their kids while they've been living in Colorado."

President Newman rubbed his forehead. "They have how many children?"

Colleen answered, "Two, a girl and a boy."

"That's right. I remember now.'

"Jimmy's the deacons quorum president, and Jenny's almost ready to graduate from Primary."

President Newman turned his attention to Randall. "Brother Simms, I want you to know how much I've appreciated your service on the high council. And the people of the third ward appreciate your service to them."

Randall nodded his head. *I'm being released.* He felt tears forming.

"But with every calling comes a release—unless you're an apostle," he chuckled.

Randall nodded his head again.

"However, with every release, comes new opportunities."

"I suppose," Randall said, barely above a whisper.

The president glanced at both of his counselors. He had a smile on his lips. "Brother Simms, are you worthy to attend the temple?"

Randall nodded his head. "We go at least once a month."

"Is there anything in your life that isn't in keeping with the teachings of the church?"

Randall thought for a moment, "No," he whispered.

"Well, Brother Simms, it is time to release Bishop Stanton. We've submitted your name to the First Presidency, received their approval, and wish to extend to you the call to serve as bishop of the first ward."

Randall nearly fell out of his chair. "You've got to be kidding? Me?"

"Absolutely, Brother Simms. I can tell you with assurance that you are the person the Lord wants to serve in that capacity."

Colleen began to sob silently. Tears rolled down her cheeks as Randall sat stunned in his chair. When she regained her composure, she turned to him and hugged him.

"Is that a 'yes'?"

Slowly Randall nodded his head. "Yes, if you're sure."

All three members of the presidency stood up with broad smiles on their faces. They shook Randall and Colleen's hands. "Congratulations," President Newman said as he took Randall's hand in his. "You'll support him?" he said to Colleen.

"Of course. You couldn't have picked a better man for the job."

"I know." He kept hold of Randall's hand. "Now, keep this to yourself. You can let your daughter know, of course. We'll make an announcement next Sunday that we're changing the bishopric the following week. That always brings a lot of people out to church. Please make a decision on your counselors as soon as possible—by Sunday at the latest. Depending upon whom you choose, there could be a domino effect in ward leadership, but the week after you're ordained is general conference. So you'll have two weeks to get everything back in order. Okay?"

Numbly, Randall nodded his head. "I'll start praying about counselors as soon as we get home."

"Good. I'll be waiting to hear from you."

Randall and Colleen walked silently to the car. Once they were headed home Colleen said, "I'm so happy for you."

"I'm glad you are. I'm overwhelmed. I never thought I'd be called as bishop."

"You'll be wonderful." She paused. "Any thoughts on who you want as counselors?"

"You know, as soon as President Newman told me he needed names, I had two people just pop into my head."

"Whoever they are, I'm sure they'd be good men to work with."

"I need to pray about it, but I really feel at peace with those two men."

CHAPTER 58

Sunday, March 21, 1999

Randall picked up the phone and called his daughter, Jill. When she answered he said, "Hello. How's my favorite daughter?"

"Dad, I'm your only daughter."

"Well, that's true. How is the rest of the Palmer clan?"

"Just great. Dan has a new calling."

"Really. What now? He's been an awfully good gospel doctrine teacher."

"Following in your footsteps; he's the new scoutmaster. Jimmy is both delighted and mortified that his dad's going to be his scoutmaster."

Randall chuckled. "He'll survive. Anyway, he turns fourteen in August and he'll move on to the varsity scouts."

"Well, Dan's hoping he can call you for some pointers. You helped so many scouts become Eagles and he'd like some pointers."

"I'd be happy to hear from him, but it's been a lot of years since I was scoutmaster."

"But I'll bet you could still give him some pointers."

"I'd be happy to do anything I can." He was quiet for a moment. "But the reason I called is that I'm being released as a high councilor next Sunday."

"Really? How come?"

"I've got a new calling."

"What?"

"Jill, I know you're going to find this hard to believe, but I've been called as bishop."

There was a moment of stunned silence before she said, "Dad, that's great. You're going to be such an awesome bishop." She covered the phone with her hand and called to her husband. Randall could hear the muffled voice as she revealed the news to her husband.

"Jill, I'm not expecting you to drop everything and come home for this, but I wanted you to know."

"Of course we'll be there, Dad. Do you still have room for the four of us?"

"You know we do. But don't put yourselves out."

"What time is your block?"

"We start at one o'clock."

"Just a minute." She covered the phone again. After a minute she said, "Dad, we'll drive up on Saturday. We ought to be there by four o'clock. Okay?"

"Wonderful. Your mother and I are excited to see you." He hung up the phone and wandered into the living room. "They're coming Saturday," he said to his wife.

"I thought they would," she said with a smile. "Now quit pacing the floor and have a seat."

"I told President Newman whom I'd like as counselors, but I haven't heard back whether they've accepted or not."

"You will." She patted the seat next to her and Randall finally sat down. "That was quite interesting at church after President Newman announced the change. It looked like everybody was looking around trying to guess who the next bishop was going to be." She chuckled as she put her arm around her husband's shoulders. "So did anyone talk to you about being bishop?"

"Nope. I don't think I'd be high on anybody's list. They all know me too well." He chuckled.

Colleen shook her head. "Randall quit that. How long are you going to dwell on past mistakes?"

Randall replied, "As long as Scotty's missing I have a daily reminder of how badly I failed as a parent. I'm not sure I'll ever put that behind me." He bowed his head. "I'd give anything to be able to put my arms around him and ask him to come home."

"Someday."

"I wish I had your faith."

CHAPTER 59

Sunday, March 28, 1999

I knew it was you," Brother Beal said as he shook Bishop Simms's hand. "Congratulations." He clapped Randall on the shoulder.

"I'm still a bit overwhelmed."

"That's to be expected."

He moved on letting the person behind him congratulate Randall. It took nearly half an hour until the crowd dispersed, and President Newman led the new bishopric and their families to the Relief Society room where he ordained Randall and set apart the other members of the bishopric.

"I'm proud of you, Dad," Jill said as she hugged him.

"Couldn't happen to a better guy," her husband, Dan, said.

"Can we go home?" his grandson, Jim, asked. "I'm hungry."

"I need to meet with Bishop Stanton for a few minutes so he can fill me in on what's going on in the ward. Jill, could you give your mother a ride home? I'll be there fairly soon."

"Sure. I guess she'll have to get used to this, won't she?"

The families moved toward the exit, and Randall opened the door to the bishop's office. Bishop Stanton was sitting behind the desk. As Randall stepped into the room, he stood up. "Well, Bishop, come and have a seat."

Randall moved slowly around the desk and sat down. He looked uncomfortable. "I don't know how I'll ever fill your shoes, Bishop."

Bishop Stanton laughed. "Oh, they're not very big. I have the feeling you'll fill them to overflowing. Maybe I can bring you up to speed on a few problems in the ward."

"Of course."

For the next half hour, the outgoing bishop explained about two families that were contemplating divorce, three who were receiving welfare assistance, and two young men who had become inactive in the last couple of months.

"I'd never have guessed," Randall said. "Any suggestions on how to help them?"

"Follow the Spirit." Bishop Stanton said softly. "As to the two divorce possibilities, I've offered counseling, but they don't seem to want it. I think there's a lot of wounded pride and stubbornness. You might have better success than I did," he said with a shrug of his shoulders. "The welfare trio; well, they're interesting. Brother Behlins is out of work and doesn't seem to want to take any job that doesn't pay him what his old job did, and they're hard to come by. Brother Andrus and Brother Call just lack job skills; they're underemployed, maybe you can work on that."

"I don't know them as well as I should. They're all elders, aren't they?"

Bishop Stanton nodded his head. "I forget that you've been out of the ward for the last three years on the high council. Which ward did you liaison with?"

"The third. Their ward meetings overlap ours, so I've only been able to attend sacrament meeting occasionally. There are a lot of people I need to learn about."

"You'll do fine. You'll be surprised how quickly you'll become acquainted with the ward members." He pointed toward the desk. "I've left a list in the drawer of the meeting schedules. Of course, you can change when you hold them—except for the block." He reached over the desk and shook Randall's hand. "I'm always here if you need me, but you're the bishop now." He reached in his pocket and took out a ring of keys. "Here you go. Since we're the last ward in the building this year, you need to make sure the doors are all locked. Oh, even though I've been released, I sent my old counselors to make the bank deposit." With a smile, he opened the door and walked out of the room.

Randall spent a few minutes familiarizing himself with the meeting schedule before turning out the lights and leaving his office. Ten minutes later, he had checked all of the doors, made sure the lights were out, and was heading home.

He parked in the garage and as he opened the kitchen door he smelled the wonderful aroma of pot roast and could hear someone playing the piano. He crossed the kitchen and entered the living room. Jill was seated at the piano playing a piece he couldn't place, while Colleen, Dan, Jim, and Jenny were listening.

Colleen spotted him, pushed herself to her feet and said, "You're home; let's eat." Jill finished playing the piano with a flourish and the six of them moved into the dining room.

"Dad, I'm so glad you bought that piano," Jill said.

Randall smiled, "Is that what your mother told you?"

"What?"

"That I bought it?"

Colleen stepped back into the dining room with the pot roast. "Well you did, sweetheart. It was bought with the quarters you contributed."

"I suppose."

"You know, 'line upon line,' quarter upon quarter, dollar upon dollar." They all burst into laughter.

When the meal was over, Jill and Colleen went to the kitchen to put the dishes in the dishwasher, while Randall and Dan returned to the living room. Jim and Jenny had spread a jigsaw puzzle on a card table and were working on it.

Dan sat down on the couch, "Randall—Dad—I've never really known what to call you, maybe bishop is more appropriate."

"Dan, you can call me anything you want, but Dad's fine."

"Well, since we're here, you had such success with your scout troop. We're struggling with ours. I'd sure appreciate some tips."

From the card table Jim said, "We never do anything."

Randall nodded his head. "I'm not sure we did anything right, but we did do a lot of things. The boys grumbled about going camping at first, but after the first couple of times, I think they looked forward to being out in the wilderness."

The conversation continued until the women joined them. Colleen said, "I was just telling Jill how thankful we were they could be here to see you ordained."

Randall nodded his head. "I'm glad you've moved back to Utah, even if you are four hours away. We've missed you. This day wouldn't have been as memorable if you hadn't been here."

"We wouldn't have missed it," Jill said. "It's not every day the family gets together for such an occasion."

Randall smiled. *It would have been complete if Scotty had been here.*

CHAPTER 60

Tuesday, July 6, 2004

andall and Colleen took their seats in front of President Newman's desk. They held hands as they waited for the president to speak.

"Bishop, as you look back over the past five years, what do you see as your successes?"

Randall hadn't been expecting that question. He thought for a moment. "Well, President, the first day as bishop I was told about two couples who were contemplating divorce. I met with them every week for several months. They're still married."

President Newman smiled as he nodded his head. "Go on."

"All but two of our priests have gone on missions. I guess that's a success, even if I didn't hit a hundred percent."

"Better than any other ward in the stake—I'm not putting anybody down, but that's a fact." President Newsman looked at the paper on his desk. "I believe you've had thirty-four young men leave on missions, along with five young women."

"President, without my counselors, none of this would have happened, but we have been able to reactivate a dozen less actives."

President Newman nodded his head again. "You've done a fantastic job." He sorted through some more papers on his desk. "But you know as well as I that with every call comes a release. I'd love to keep you as bishop forever, but it's time we give someone else a chance for all those blessings. We'll be in your ward next Sunday to announce that a new bishopric is being called."

Colleen squeezed Randall's hand. He nodded his head. "I suspected it was about time. These five years have gone by too quickly. There's still a lot of work to be done, but I'm sure whoever replaces me can handle that."

President Newman stood up, walked around his desk, and hugged Randall. "Bishop, you're going to be a tough act to follow." He took Colleen's hand in his. "What a support you have been; never a negative word."

"I've tried my best," she said softly. "But it will be good to be able to sit with him in church again."

President Newman nodded his head. "Any regrets?"

"Not really. No one's perfect, but my husband comes pretty close."

"I agree." He opened the door and ushered them out of his office. "Thank you both."

Randall and Colleen walked out into the warm summer night. A few fireworks left over from the Fourth of July were exploding in the sky. Silently, they reached the car and sat down on the seat. Randall rolled down the windows and let the faint breeze glide through the car. "Well, sweetheart, I knew this day was coming, but it's still a bit of a shock."

Colleen rubbed the back of her husband's neck. "President Newman was right—you're going to be a tough act to follow."

"That's not true. Whoever the Lord wants, he'll help."

Randall started the car and pulled out of the parking lot. Colleen continued to massage his neck. "Randall, I hope this doesn't make you upset but I'd like to tell you something."

"Okay."

"Do you know the biggest change I've seen in you since we got married?"

He smiled. "Less hair and more stomach?"

"Well, I suppose that's true, but not what I had in mind." She paused. "I hope you don't take offense."

"I won't."

"Okay. When we were first married you always tried to outdo the other guy."

"I always tried to do my best," he interrupted.

"You still do; but at first I think it was so you could show up the competition."

"Oh, I . . ."

"Just let me finish. You still do an amazing job of anything you set your mind to, but not to show up anybody—just because you want to do the best job you can do. There's no competition any more; just excellence for excellence's sake." She gave his neck one more rub. "I mean that as a compliment. Please take it that way."

They drove silently for a couple of blocks before Randall replied, "Thank you. Maybe I've grown up a little bit."

"I love you. You've been a great bishop and a greater husband and father."

"Maybe to Jill. Then there's Scott."

After a moment of silence, Colleen said, "I wish we knew where he is and what he's doing."

They pulled into the driveway and climbed out of the car. "Have you ever thought he might have died?"

Colleen shook her head, "No. Someday he'll return. I just feel it so strongly."

"Well, I hope I'm alive to see him."

Colleen linked her arm through Randall's, "I think that is a two-way street."

CHAPTER 61

A re you ready?" Randall called out.

"Just a minute. I'm just finishing my hair."

"We're going to be late."

"Sweetheart, church doesn't start for an hour."

Randall shook his head, "It starts at ten o'clock. And it's five minutes to ten."

Colleen tucked a final strand of hair into place. "Randall, church starts at eleven." She glanced at the calendar hanging on the wall above the phone. *June 20—the fifth anniversary of Jill and Dan moving to Bountiful.*

"When did they change? Don't they usually change at the first of the year?"

Colleen seated herself on the couch next to her husband. "It did change in January. And last year we started at eight o'clock. We've never started at ten."

Randall shook his head. "It was always at ten when I was bishop." He pushed himself up from the couch, plunked himself down in his recliner and reached for the newspaper.

Colleen took a deep breath. "Are you going to wear a tie to church?"

Randall reached for his throat. "I guess I forgot that." He launched himself out of the recliner and marched to his bedroom.

Ten minutes passed before Colleen called out, "Do you need help?" When there was no response, she hurried to the bedroom. Randall was curled up on the bed, fast asleep.

Colleen decided to wait half an hour before waking him. She made her way to the kitchen, where she boiled some water and made Jell-O for dinner. She was putting in the refrigerator when she heard the front door open and close.

She looked out the window in time to see Randall walk slowly down the street. He was moving as if in a dream. He reached the corner before his wife jogged to his side.

"Where are you going?" she asked as she took hold of his arm.

"To the store." His lips tightened. "Don't you remember you wanted me to get some cheese?"

Colleen took a deep breath before she answered. "Randall, that was nearly a week ago. Don't you remember we went shopping last Wednesday?"

Randall looked slightly confused. "Are you sure? Isn't today Wednesday?"

"No, sweetheart, it's Sunday. Church starts in about fifteen minutes. Let's go home and get your tie and jacket so we're not late."

He shook his head. "Are you sure?" he said again.

She nodded her head. "I'm sure." She guided him back up the street to their home, led him through the front door, and helped him put on a tie.

"When does church start?" he asked.

"In about ten minutes. We'd better get moving."

They stepped into the garage and Randall started to get into the driver's side of the car when Colleen said, "Why don't you let me drive."

"I always drive," he said somewhat angrily.

"I know, but why don't you rest and let me drive for a change."

He shrugged his shoulders and handed her the keys. They reached the chapel with less than a minute to spare.

"Brother Simms, how are you?" Bishop Crawford stood at the door greeting the congregation.

"Fine," Randall mumbled as he wandered down the aisle. Colleen grabbed his arm and led him to a vacant seat. "Who was that?" Randall asked.

"Bishop Crawford, our new bishop. Don't you remember? He was sustained about two months ago."

Randall shook his head. "Never saw him before."

Colleen bowed her head. *I think this ride's getting rougher. There may be some things that are worse than death.*

Randall craned his neck as he looked around the chapel. "This is a really pretty building," he said, "Whose house is this anyway?"

PART FOUR

Redemption

CHAPTER 62

Saturday, December 19, 2015

Scott bowed his head as Gordon dedicated the grave. The family sat beneath a green shade shelter that had been erected at the grave site. Snow glistened around the freshly dug grave. Scott had been enlisted as a pallbearer. He removed the white carnation from his lapel and placed it on top of the casket along with the rest of the pallbearers. He returned to his seat next to his mother. Jill and her children sat on the other side.

At his mother's bidding, he pushed her wheelchair as close to the casket as he could. She leaned forward, placed her hands on the polished walnut, and wept. After a moment, she straightened up and asked Scott to pull her back under the canopy. Once she was in place, the dedicatory ceremony began.

After the grave was dedicated, Bishop Crawford stepped to the portable microphone. "That concludes the services. We appreciate all of you who have been here to support Colleen and her family. The Relief Society has prepared a lunch for the family back at the chapel."

The congregation of mourners began to disperse to their cars, many of them pausing to offer condolences. Scott was amazed at the number of people who had come to honor his father. He was still trying to come to grips with the fact his father had served as bishop.

Richard Newman approached the family. "I'm sure you've heard these words before, but if there is anything Penny and I can do, please don't hesitate to call on us."

"I appreciate that, President. I think we're going to be just fine." Colleen smiled at him from her wheelchair. "You were such a great stake president. Randall just couldn't say enough good things about you."

"You're too kind." His gaze wandered through the trees that ringed the cemetery. "These last few years must have been trying."

She nodded her head.

"Well, don't feel guilty. You took care of Bishop Simms better than anyone else could have done." He took her hand in his. "He was such a good man, but your support was equally impressive." He turned to Scott, "Are you still going to be here Monday?"

"I think so."

"I'd like to take you to lunch and share old times. I have hospital rounds to do in the morning, but if you're available about one o'clock, I'll swing by and pick you up. Okay?"

Scott nodded his head. "That would be great. Last night you mentioned Swenson's. It's still there?" President Newman nodded his head. The last of the mourners made their way to their cars.

CHAPTER 63

Sunday, December 20, 2015

Scott rolled the wheelchair into a spot between two sections of seating at the back of the chapel and sat down next to his mother. The organist was playing "The First Noel" for the prelude music. When she finished, Bishop Crawford stepped to the pulpit. Just as he began to speak, Jill and her children slid in next to Scott.

"Brothers and Sisters, welcome. My name is James Crawford, I'm the bishop of the first ward. We have prepared a wonderful program for you today. But before we begin there are a few announcements." He spoke of several events that were coming up in the next couple of weeks, then concluded by saying, "We extend out condolences to Sister Colleen Simms and her family. As most of you know, Brother Randall passed away earlier this week."

The opening hymn was sung and the invocation given. After some ward business was conducted, the sacrament was blessed and passed. When it was offered to Scott, he contemplated whether he should take it or not, but when he saw his mother smiling at him, he took the bread and water.

Bishop Crawford stood again. "Brothers and sisters, the ward choir will now favor us with "Angels We Have Heard on High.""

After the choir finished singing their number, Sister Sanders made her way to the microphone. "Without Easter there was no need for Christmas; and without Christmas there is no need for Easter. But at this time of year when we celebrate the birth of the Only Begotten of the Father, we pave the way to his great atoning sacrifice, his death, and resurrection." She unfolded a sheet of paper and read,

> She with child and not yet wed,
> The thought had filled his heart with dread,
> In spite of what the angel said.
> Oh, what a trip it was for them,
> That eighty miles to Bethlehem.
>
> And how much did the mother know
> Of the road her child would go?
> 'A sword shall pierce thy soul also.'
> Oh, what a trip it was for them,
> That eighty miles to Bethlehem.
>
> This Child, the First Born of the Lord
> Would teach by action and with word;
> Then suffer lash and nail and sword.
> Oh, what a trip it was for them,
> That eighty miles to Bethlehem.
>
> They traveled on, this holy three
> To the focal point of history,
> The tomb, the cross, Gethsemane.
> Oh, what a trip it was for them,
> That four score miles to Bethlehem.

Sister Sanders dabbed at her cheek with a tissue. "So here we stand at this time of year contemplating the greatest gift of all—the birth of our Lord and Savior Jesus Christ." She spoke for a few more minutes before bearing her testimony and returning to her seat.

The choir rose and sang, "When blossoms flowered 'mid the snows, upon a winter night." Scott felt a welling of emotion within him that he hadn't felt in years. When the flute joined in, tears sprang unbidden to his eyes. The choir concluded the number and sat down. Brother McKay stood at the pulpit.

"Brothers and sisters, this is a wonderful time of the year. It is a time of giving. Children wait for Christmas morning and the gifts spread around the Christmas tree. Santa Claus rarely disappoints. There is nothing wrong with this. It is a time of giving. But more important is the gift of salvation given by a loving Heavenly Father through the birth of his Son. The choir has just sung about the Christmas Rose—a symbol of our Savior—the King of love and light."

He spoke for another five minutes before taking his seat.

The rest of the meeting went as had been announced. Scott found it hard to join with the choir as they concluded with "Silent Night." The feelings he was feeling were too intense. An ocean full of guilt threatened to drown him, but as tears rolled down his cheeks he felt his mother's hand close over his. A feeling of peace washed over him.

He turned to his sister and whispered, "I'm so sorry. Can you ever forgive me?"

Before she could answer, another sister stepped to the microphone and began offering the benediction.

Chapter 64

Sunday, December 20, 2015

Scott wheeled his mother into the living room. A wonderful aroma of dinner wafted from the kitchen. "What do I smell?"

"The Relief Society has brought over dinner," his mother said with a smile. "Have a seat, Scotty." He sank down onto the couch as she cleared her throat. "You seemed touched by the Christmas program."

He nodded his head. "I don't know what came over me. I haven't felt that way in years."

She sat silently while her son looked at the Christmas tree. The lights on the star blinked on and off. "The music was beautiful."

"Yes, yes it was." They sat quietly for several minutes. "I asked Jill to forgive me," he said in a whisper.

Colleen smiled. "And what did she say?"

Scott shook his head. "Nothing."

"Really?"

"Well, it was just before they said the closing prayer."

"I see. It might take a little while for that to happen."

"I know." He pushed himself off the couch and knelt down next to his mother. "Mom, I've made a lot of mistakes in my life."

Before he could say more, she laid her hand on his shoulder. "But nothing can change those things. Scott, focus on the future."

"I'm not sure what the future looks like."

Colleen patted his shoulder. "Well, you're the one who has to decide." She paused. "Are you happy with what you're doing in Keokuk?"

He shrugged his shoulders. "I don't know. I thought I was, but there's really not a lot keeping me there." Thoughts of Charese rose unbidden to his mind. Despair wrapped itself around him like a suffocating cocoon.

Colleen took a deep breath before speaking, "We'd love to have you come home. There's always room for you here."

Scott nodded his head. "I'm a little old to be starting over."

"Oh, Scott," she started to say, but stopped and waited for him to continue.

"Mom, what would I do? I mean, it may not be much, but I am managing a Walmart."

"Would they transfer you here?"

"I don't know," he said. Colleen rose and went back to the couch.

"Well, let's eat dinner. I don't know what Sister Savage brought over, but it smells heavenly."

While they were eating Scott said, "I think this is what I miss the most—neighbors helping neighbors." His mother smiled a knowing smile. "I think I'll call the home office tomorrow and see if there's any chance of relocating to Utah."

CHAPTER 65

Monday, December 21, 2015

Scott called out to his mother, "You're going to be all right?"

"Yes, dear. Go catch up with President Newman."

"If you're sure." He heard the horn honk in the driveway. Scott let himself out of the house and walked down the sidewalk to where Richard Newman sat in his black Lincoln MKZ. He slid into the passenger's seat.

Richard shook Scott's hand. "Buckle up, old buddy. Let's go get some lunch."

"So, Swenson's? Scott asked.

"Yup." Richard backed out of the driveway and headed down the road toward the center of town. Swenson's had occupied its spot in the middle of town for over seventy-five years. The menu had changed over time, but they were still known for their pies and homemade ice cream.

Richard pulled into the parking lot and the two of them entered the building. It was as if time had stood still. Without any direction, they went to their favorite booth and slid onto the Naugahyde covered seats.

A young blond girl approached them. "Do you need menus?" she asked.

Richard shook his head. "I'll have the chicken fried steak and a Fresca."

"Sounds good, I'll have the same," Scott said.

"I'll get it right up," she said with a smile.

Scott watched her walk away. "Remember Joy?"

Richard nodded his head and smiled. "She took wonderful care of us, even when we were rowdy little punks."

"She was a great waitress. I wonder what happened to her?"

"She moved to Brigham City a long time ago. That's her grand-daughter who waited on us."

"You're kidding me."

"Nope. Joy's daughter, Hope, took over the place when Joy and her husband moved. Now Hope is fighting cancer and Jean has taken over. Her eighty-year-old aunt still runs the kitchen."

"That's Jean?" Scott said pointing at their waitress.

"Yup."

"She's not old enough to be running a restaurant."

"She's twenty-five."

"That's pretty young."

Jean returned with their Frescas. "Food will be here in a minute."

Richard winked at her. "Thanks, Jean." He turned his attention back to Scott. "So. Where did you go? Where have you been?"

"It's a long story. And maybe not a very happy one."

"I've got time. I don't have appointments for two hours."

Scott took a deep breath and began with the arguments he and his father had had. He had just made it to Sacramento when Jean returned with their food. "Keep room for dessert," she said as she slipped the plates onto the table.

Before Scott continued, Richard said, "You know, your father made some pretty big changes in his life after you left."

"So I gather. It's hard for me to believe he was a bishop."

"Probably as hard to believe as me being a stake president."

Scott shook his head. "We did do some pretty dumb things, didn't we?"

"Yes we did." He smiled. "Thankfully nothing we couldn't be forgiven for."

Scott's brow furrowed. "You know I'm not sure I ever realized that until yesterday. It was as if sacrament meeting was aimed directly at me."

"Why?"

"It was all about being forgiven. About the Atonement."

"You know something, Scott, I'm sure you aren't the only person who feels that way. All of us have things in our past we'd like to forget—or be given a do over."

Between bites of food, Scott continued telling his old friend about some of the life he'd lived. He finished his story just as Jean approached them.

"Well, gentlemen, did you save room for pie?"

Richard patted his stomach. "There's always room for pie and ice cream. Do you have any cherry?"

"Of course, Dr. Newman—heated, with a scoop of vanilla ice cream, if I remember right."

"Oh, you have a good memory, Jean." He cocked an eyebrow toward Scott. "What about you?"

"What about a chocolate banana malt?"

"Coming right up."

Richard smiled. "Just like old times."

"Speaking of forgiveness, I see you're still eating pie. Remember that family reunion where you ate all the pies?"

Richard smiled. "I was only fourteen. You do have a good memory."

Scott raised an eyebrow. "Sometimes too good." He looked down at the tabletop and sighed.

"Well, little did I know what would come of that reunion."

"Oh? What?"

"You met my wife, Penny, at the viewing."

"Yes, she's beautiful."

"I'll tell her you said that. She was my cousin Maria's roommate at Rick's College. That's how we met. Maria introduced us."

Scott looked confused.

"Maria was the shirttail third cousin I met at the reunion. When she beat me in the sack race, I tackled her and got kissed in return."

Scott nodded his head. "Oh, yeah, I remember, now."

The pie and malt arrived.

"What about you, Scott. How come you've never married?"

Scott inspected the tabletop as he answered, "That's part of the story I didn't tell you." Richard waited for Scott to continue, but he sat silently in the booth.

When they'd finished dessert, Richard caught Jean's eye. She dropped off the bill. Richard reached in his wallet and left her a generous tip. "I need to get back to the office pretty soon." As an afterthought he asked, "Would you like to see where I work?"

"Sure."

Five minutes later they took the elevator to the fourth floor of the medical building and walked into Richard's reception area. The receptionist greeted them warmly.

"Dr. Newman, your two o'clock appointment is going to be a few minutes late. She just called."

"Thanks, Christy, this is my old friend, Scott Simms."

"Pleased to meet you. Are you Randall's son?" Scott nodded his head. "I'm so sorry to hear about your father's passing."

"Thank you," Scott managed to say. Richard led him down a short hallway to his office and gestured toward a leather love seat that sat under a window.

"Have a seat."

CHAPTER 66

Monday, December 21, 2015

Richard, tell me about my father. You called him as bishop, didn't you?"

Richard Newman sat down in the swivel chair behind his desk. "In a sense I called him, but really the Lord called him and I was just the mouthpiece."

"Okay, I get that, but why my father?"

"The Lord wanted him."

"Richard, you knew my father almost as well as your own. Can you understand why I'm having such a hard time understanding this whole thing?"

Richard leaned back in his chair and swiveled back and forth for a moment. "Scott, I'm going to try to explain this as best I can and then I'm going to share something with you that you might find hard to believe. Okay?" Scott nodded his head.

"When we were kids growing up, I thought your father was about the strictest and meanest man I'd ever met. When you were grounded for a month after the pig incident, I thought the punishment far exceeded the crime, and I felt pretty good about what my father did to me."

"That wasn't one of the high points of our high school years, for sure."

Richard chuckled. "Thank heavens for repentance." He leaned forward and put his hands on the desktop. "Then you left. Why? I didn't know, but I watched what happened to your family. Each one of them handled it differently. Your mother suffered in silence. Your sister just couldn't understand where you'd gone. But your father roamed up and down the streets looking for you. When he came to our house asking if I'd seen you, I saw a man who was worried, but still defiant."

"He always had to be in charge," Scott said, shaking his head.

"Perhaps. Then I went away to college and a mission. When I returned, your father seemed like a different man. He appeared to really want to know how my mission had gone. Something had changed him, and he continued to change."

"Do you know about the quarters in the jar?"

Richard shook his head. "No. What about them?"

"It's not important. I've interrupted you, go on."

"Well, I went away to school and finally came home after I'd finished my residency. That meant that the only time I'd seen your father was when I was home for short vacations. I really didn't spend much time with him, except I always asked him if he'd heard from you."

"Which of course he hadn't."

"No. But when I finally established my practice here in Bountiful, Penny and I bought a home in our old neighborhood. Brother Fullmer had died and his widow wasn't able to take care of the house. Anyway, we bought their home and remodeled it. So, we were back in the old ward."

"How long did it take to become a doctor?"

"Ten years. Anyway, when we went to church, your father was always there early, straightening things up. Whenever he'd see me he'd hurry over and give me a hug."

Scott rolled his eyes. "That must have been a shock. I never saw him hug anyone."

"That was a time of many shocks. I'd barely established my practice before I received a call as stake president."

"When was that?"

"March of 1998. We'd been home less than three years."

"That must have been a surprise. You were pretty young."

Richard smiled. "Yes I was; thankfully I had counselors who were a little older and much more seasoned that I was. Anyway, when we held our first high council meeting, there was your father. He'd been serving for a couple of years as the liaison with the third ward. To be honest, I was a little surprised to see him on the council. I still held to preconceived notions; but he was as faithful as anyone I've ever seen. He was totally and completely dedicated to his calling."

Richard paused as someone knocked on the door. He stood up and cracked it open. "Give me ten more minutes," he said. He turned back to Scott. "My next appointment is here. I guess I need to speed up a bit."

"Look, I can go and let you get on with your patients. We can talk later."

"No, that's all right. This won't take much longer." He sat back down. "A year later it was time to release the bishop in the first ward. My counselors and I printed out a list of all the Melchizedek Priesthood holders. We each took a copy and went home to ponder and pray. The next time we met, we all had the same name at the top of our list—Randall Simms. So, we submitted the name to the First Presidency—they have to approve the submitted name before they can be called. The letter came back approving our submission. So, your father was recommended by us and sustained by the First Presidency. I extended the call." Richard nodded his head. "That's how it happened."

"Remarkable. I'm still trying to reconcile the man I knew with what you've said."

Richard stood up, walked around the desk, and hugged his friend. "I told you there was something I needed to tell you."

"What?"

"Every time I met with your father for an interview he'd always say, 'My greatest regret is not being able to beg my son's forgiveness.' And he'd cry."

Scott's eyes flew open. "He wanted to beg my forgiveness?"

Richard nodded his head. "He was deeply sorry he'd driven you away."

The impact of that statement forced Scott to sink back down on the love seat. Tears began to roll down his cheeks. "Oh, Richard, I've been so stupid, so wrong. I blamed him for everything, but I was just as guilty. Now that he's gone . . . it's too late."

Richard put his arm around his friend's shoulders. "There will come a time. After all, families can be together forever."

"I feel so empty. So alone."

"You're never alone, Scott."

"Yesterday in church, it was as if they'd planned the meeting just for me. I haven't felt the Spirit like that in years."

"Maybe there's a message there."

"What can I do? How can I make up what I've done to my mother and my sister?"

There was a knock on the door. Richard opened it and held up his hand with the fingers spread. "Five more minutes," he said to his receptionist before he placed his hand on his friend's shoulder. "Scott, let them know how you feel. It will take time, but it can happen."

Scott heaved himself to his feet. "I need to get out of here and let you take care of your patients."

Richard put his hand on his friend's shoulder. "Would you like me to give you a blessing?"

"You'd do that? Even knowing all about what I've done?"

"Of course." He paused. "I feel confident you're about to make some amends for whatever is needed." He helped Scott sit down on the chair next to his desk. He placed his hands on Scott's head. "What's your full name?"

"Randall Scott Simms."

And the blessing began.

Chapter 67

Sunday, June 5, 2016

Fast and testimony meeting came to a close. As usual, two people had hurried to the stand at the last minute and borne their testimonies, so the meeting had gone a few minutes over. Scott sat next to his mother in one of the benches on the south side of the chapel. Jill sat on her other side. The meeting had been inspirational. Of course, half a dozen children had hurried to the stand and assured the congregation that their families loved them, but Brother Okotie-Eboh's testimony had resonated in Scott's heart. A recent convert to the church from Nigeria, he had moved to Bountiful after accepting a position as a custodian at the University of Utah, although he'd been a successful businessman in Africa. His humble, powerful testimony brought tears to Scott's eyes. He had given up everything and yet his testimony was unwavering.

Scott offered his hand to his mother and pulled her gently to her feet. The wheelchair had been left behind months ago, but she still struggled with a bit of pain after sitting for long periods of time.

The three of them made their way to the foyer. "Are you coming over for dinner?" Scott asked his sister.

Jill nodded her head. "I'm going to run home and change clothes first."

Colleen tightened her grip on Scott's arm and winked her eye at him. "There's no need to hurry. Dinner won't be ready for an hour or so."

Bishop Crawford put his hand on Scott's shoulder. "Do you have a minute, Brother Simms?"

Scott looked at his mother. "Sure, Bishop. Should I run Mom home first?"

Bishop Crawford shook his head. "This will only take a moment." He turned to Colleen. "Can I steal him for a couple of minutes?"

Colleen nodded her head, "I'll just wait on the couch." She crossed the foyer and seated herself slowly while Scott and the bishop entered the office.

"Have a seat," the bishop said as he made his way around his desk.

Scott sat down, crossed his legs, and nervously interlaced his fingers. The bishop smiled at him. "So, how are things going, Brother Simms?"

"Okay, I guess."

"How's your mother doing? Still grieving, I suppose."

Scott began to relax. "Oh, she has her moments, but I think she's actually relieved Dad isn't suffering anymore. And her hip seems to have healed pretty well."

Bishop Crawford nodded his head. "Good, good. And how's Jill?"

Scott looked down at the carpet in front of him for a moment before answering. "I guess she's okay."

The bishop waited patiently.

"It's been hard, but I think she's forgiven me."

"Brother Simms, I know how hard it was for you to come in and talk with me after you made the decision to come home, but it appears things have worked out pretty well."

Scott bowed his head and examined the carpet in front of him. "Bishop, telling you what I'd done was probably the hardest thing

I've ever had to do. I was sure you were going to throw me out of the church."

Bishop Crawford smiled. "You might find this hard to believe, but I've heard worse things."

"Really?"

The bishop nodded his head. "How have things worked out?"

Scott looked out the window before he turned his head and looked at the bishop. "Well, I found out my first wife divorced me. After I left, she waited nearly five years before she had our marriage dissolved. She claimed desertion." He felt tears running down his cheeks. "I don't know how I can ever expect her to forgive me for being so dishonest with her."

Bishop Crawford nodded his head again. "Do you know what else has happened to her?"

"She remarried and has three children," he said softly.

"So things seem to have worked out for her."

"I suppose. My second wife has moved on as well. I guess there's some question as to whether we were ever legally married."

"Do you know how she's doing?"

"I've written to her and begged her forgiveness. I'm not expecting miracles."

"But she answered?"

Scott nodded his head. "She's still pretty angry. I don't blame her."

They sat silently for another minute or two before Bishop Crawford said, "How have things worked out with Walmart?"

Scott shook his head. "It was quite a mess. I mean, they were willing to have Craig Spillman transfer to the Centerville store, but they weren't so sure about Scott Simms."

Bishop Crawford chuckled, "I'll bet that was an interesting conversation."

Scott shrugged his shoulders. "Anyway, we've worked it out. I'm pretty happy with the move. Of course, I'm not the manager, but at least I'm employed. And Craig Spillman is buried for good."

"Good." The bishop smiled. "Well, Brother Simms, you've done everything I've asked you to do. I think you've tried to make amends for everything in your past. It has been so good to see you here every Sunday. You seem so much happier than when you first visited with me. I think it's time to get you ordained an elder."

Scott's eyes flew open. "So soon? I mean, it has only been six months."

The bishop nodded his head. "I'm sure. I've made the recommendation to President Conway and he agrees. He'll be contacting you for an interview this week. Once you're ordained, let's set a date for the temple. We need to get you endowed . . . and sealed to your parents. I think your father's waiting."

Scott's shoulders shook as he felt tears streaming down his cheeks. "Bishop, I don't know how to thank you."

"I've done nothing. It's you, Scott, who's made a remarkable transition." He left his desk, took Scott by both hands, and lifted him to his feet. The two men hugged.

"Thank you," Scott said.

"Oh, there is one more thing."

Scott took a deep breath, "What else do I need to do?" he whispered.

"I wonder if you'd serve on the Fourth of July breakfast committee?"

"Of course," Scott laughed.

"It's the elders quorum's turn and you're going to be the newest elder. Brother Snyder, the elders quorum president, will be contacting you. They have a meeting Tuesday night."

Scott shook the bishop's hand, wiped the tears from his cheeks, stepped out of the office, and crossed the foyer to where his mother sat on the couch. "Let's go home," he said as he lifted her to her feet.

His mother took his hand and the two of them walked out of the church. As he slid into the driver's seat, Scott saw Bishop Crawford smile and wave at him through the door of the chapel.

"Mom, they're going to make me an elder."

Colleen smiled broadly. "That's wonderful. You deserve it."

"Maybe." Scott tightened his grip on the steering wheel. "And I'm going to be on the Fourth of July breakfast committee."

Colleen laughed out loud. "Like father, like son."

In so many ways, Scott thought.

DISCUSSION QUESTIONS

1. Why do two people who experience the same event see it so differently?

2. Do you think Colleen is accurate when she says change must come from within the person him or herself?

3. What opportunities did Scott pass up by making the choices he made?

4. Why was Jill so angry with her brother?

ABOUT THE AUTHOR

Richard M. Siddoway was born in Salt Lake City and reared in Bountiful, Utah. He was a professional educator for over forty-five years. In 1994, he was asked by Governor Leavitt to create the nation's first statewide virtual high school—The Electronic High School—which served students nationwide.

He served three terms in the Utah House of Representatives; the last two years he served as Speaker Pro Tempore of the House. Fulfilling a promise to his electorate, he limited his service to three terms.

He has served as a bishop and stake president in the Bountiful Utah Val Verda Stake. He and his wife, Janice, are the parents of eight children and grandparents of twenty-six grandchildren. They have served missions in Nauvoo, Illinois, and Taylorsville, Utah.

Richard is the author of eleven previous books, including the *New York Times* best-seller *The Christmas Wish*, which was made into a movie starring Debbie Reynolds, Neil Patrick Harris, and Naomi Watts.

SCAN TO VISIT

WWW.SIDDOWAY.ORG